BONES AND THE SMILING MACKEREL

Funk & Wagnalls Company, Inc.   New York

BONES and the SMILING MACKEREL

by *Jean Caryl*

Illustrated by Jessica Zemsky

FOR MURIEL AND IRA

Contents

BONES AND THE SMILING MACKEREL

1. Grand Central Station

Boniface Cluett, nicknamed Bones, at twelve years and five months, had to hold his breath to button his size-sixteen "husky" shorts. He looked down at his knees. He was mortified.

"Dimpled grapefruits!" he exclaimed. "I never said I wanted to go to camp, and if it means wearing shorts, count me out!"

His father drummed the folded newspaper on his lap. "Don't worry about your knees. They're just temporary —I mean the fat. The camp will put you on a diet and see that you stick to it. With all the swimming and sports, your flesh will consolidate."

"My flesh will what?" Bones asked. "This is impossible!

I can't walk through Grand Central Station in these, and besides this is an arty camp. They don't even have hard ball. What kind of exercise do you expect me to get at Camp Crescendo, 'the haven consecrated to culture'?" In desperation, he tugged at a strand of his light brown hair.

"Don't believe everything you read in the folders. Where there's a gang of boys, there'll be exercise—soccer, basketball, relay races—"

"Relay races," interrupted Bones in disgust. "That's for skinny guys. Why can't I stay home? Shorehaven is great in the summer. I can swim in the Sound and play baseball. It's much cheaper."

Mr. Cluett sighed. "You're enrolled. I've paid your tuition."

Bones's older sister, Carolyn, entered the living room, trim in her pleated tennis dress. She sprawled out on the sofa, dangling one slim leg over the arm. "You had no objection to Camp Crescendo till you tried on those shorts!" She snickered. "Not that I blame you."

Bones stuck his tongue out at Carolyn. He wished she would leave him alone. "Whitey kind of talked me into it." He sighed. "Whitey said camp was great, not a bit like what parents expected. You know—cookouts, overnight hikes, gooey desserts, and funny plays. There's another thing, too," he continued, looking at his dad. "I really don't want to play your trombone at camp. I like my guitar. It's not my fault they don't use guitars in bands or orchestras."

"You can take your guitar," his father told him, "but your mother and I feel you should learn something new."

Carolyn winked at Bones.

"You're trying to shape me into a skinny egghead, a

boney Bones," he protested. "Whitey should have been your son. He can play the flute and sing on key. He can even paint so it looks like something."

Mr. Cluett chuckled. "Basically, Bones, I like you the way you are. I just want to change a few incidentals."

"Incidentals!" retorted Bones with indignation. "It feels like spring cleaning!"

The telephone rang.

Midge, Bones's seven-year-old sister, called from upstairs. "Boney, telephone."

Bones went to the hall phone. "Whitey . . . Yeah . . . How do those shorts look on you? . . . You don't say . . . Ho! Ho!" Bones laughed. "I get it," he said and hung up.

"What's new with Whitey?" Mr. Cluett asked searchingly.

"Nothing much," Bones replied and changed the subject.

The rest of the week before camp started, Bones was too busy playing baseball to think or talk much about the approaching summer. He realized that his parents steered clear of the subject so that he would not have an opportunity to raise further objections. Every now and then Mrs. Cluett would look at him and sigh. She had misgivings, too, Bones decided, but she did not voice them.

The night before he was to leave, he oiled his mitt and stowed it on his bookshelf. It was the last thing he looked at the next morning as he left his room. With a heavy heart he joined his parents and Midge in the family car, bound for the Shorehaven Railroad Station.

When the local train from Shorehaven arrived in Grand Central Terminal, Mr. Cluett helped Bones on with his knapsack. "What's in here, anyway, your rock collection?"

"Just odds and ends. Things I'll be needing."

"Like what?" Mr. Cluett pursued.

"Like stuff to read on the train, and junk. You know."

Mr. Cluett shook his head. "Feels like a set of encyclopedias, but more likely it's a ten-year supply of comics."

Bones made no reply, but he grinned, thinking of the dungarees Whitey had suggested he pack, and the two-pound box of homemade fudge his Grandmother Twiggly had slipped him the night before.

As he walked down the ramp, Bones made Midge keep in front of him. With his guitar case hiding one side, and his sister landscaping the other, his knees might not be too conspicuous.

The Friday morning commuting crowd converged with the marching campers and parents. Bones thought his mother looked silly trying to keep up with him, wearing high heels and juggling his fishing rod. She apologized as she hooked a commuter's attaché case. "It's hot," Mrs. Cluett said when she reached Bones. "You're lucky to be wearing shorts."

"Lucky!" snorted Bones. But then he realized that mothers never thought their sons looked grotesque.

Bones had to slow down to walk with his mother.

"It's going to be a wonderful summer for you," Mrs. Cluett said. "Mrs. Duff has been telling me all about Crescendo. They offer so much in all the arts, and they have a marvelous staff."

Bones did not reply. Whitey's grandmother might have convinced Mr. and Mrs. Cluett of the merits of Camp Crescendo, Bones thought, but she hadn't impressed him. The more he thought about it, the more disgusted he became with himself for having been talked into a camp without a baseball diamond, a camp whose virtues bored him. What did he care about music, art, and drama? He must have been crazy when he let Whitey persuade him to go to camp.

Mrs. Cluett's tight skirt prevented her from matching Bones's gait. Her son had to meet her pace, and climbing the stairs to the upper level of the terminal became a snail-like ordeal. Bones was not surprised when they found themselves separated from the rest of his family. "Now what?" he asked, when it was evident that they had lost his father and Midge.

"What was the name of that train? The Symphony Special?"

"The South Hill Special." Bones let out a deep breath. Symphonies, operettas, sculpting, singing—that's all his parents talked about lately. They expected him to inhale culture in South Hill, Vermont, the site of Camp Crescendo, and they expected him to exhale pounds.

Mrs. Duff, Whitey Duff's grandmother, hailed them. "Follow us," she called. "I know the way."

Whitey led the group by maneuvering his flute case through the mob. The others followed.

Bones found Midge sitting on his suitcase in front of the sign: *Camp Crescendo, The South Hill Special*.

"Where's Dad?" Bones inquired.

"Looking for you," replied Midge. "He told me not to move for anything."

"Hello, Midge," said Mrs. Duff. "You going to visit me while the boys are away?"

"Um, hmm." Then Midge burst into tears.

Mrs. Cluett tried to comfort her by saying, "Carolyn will be home this summer, and later on we're going to Vermont to visit Bones."

"I know." Midge started to cry again. "Oh, Boney, don't go away," she said between sobs.

"Believe me, Midge, I'd rather stay home, but it's too

late to turn back now. Right, Whitey?" He sought confirmation from the tow-headed boy who stood beside his grandmother. Bones put his finger under Midge's chin and stooped to whisper in her ear.

Midge smiled. Then she sponged her tears with her organdy sash and said, "Don't forget the surprise."

"That reminds me," said Mrs. Cluett, opening her pocketbook. "Your big sister didn't forget you either, even if she's sleeping now." She handed Bones a package that felt like a book. "Carolyn said you should open this on the train."

It felt heavy. Maybe his sister had bought him the *Sports Encyclopedia* he had been wanting.

The conductor opened the iron gates. Carrying instruments, knapsacks, and suitcases, girls and boys, from eight through sixteen years of age, sweated past the doors that led to the train.

Mr. Cluett returned with an armload of comic books and chewing gum. "It's a long ride," he explained.

Hoards of campers were pushing past them. Some wore the camp uniform—pine-needle green shorts and white polo shirts with the Camp Crescendo emblem. Others were dressed as they wished—girls in gay blouses and skirts, boys with crew-cut heads wearing khaki pants or chinos.

"I'd better find these kids some seats," Bones's father said to the ladies and Midge. "You three wait here. It's steaming down there."

Bones tensed with excitement at all the new faces. He had plenty of friends at home, but camp would be a test —a test in getting on with strangers. Whitey's presence was a comfort, but Whitey was at home in the music world. He would move on familiar territory at Camp Crescendo, while Bones anticipated looking like a hamster in a fish tank. The expression on his mother's face did not add to his ease. He felt as if he were being sent to prison. But she kissed him and said, "Have fun! Have a wonderful summer, and please write!"

2. The South Hill Special

Mr. Cluett stacked the guitar, trombone, and flute on the rack above the seats, while the boys slid off their knapsacks.

"We'll leave these down here," Bones said quickly, catching Whitey's eye.

"You'll need a camel to drag this gear." Mr. Cluett placed the suitcase beside the instruments and shook his head.

"Bones! Bones!" They could hear Mrs. Cluett calling, but they couldn't see her until Midge shrieked, "There he is!"

Then they saw the fishing rod waving above the heads of campers and parents.

"Stay where you are, boys," said Mr. Cluett. "I'll get it."

"All aboard," the conductor shouted.

"It's about time," declared Whitey. "This is the worst part of the trip."

The conductor started to shut the doors.

With one foot on the platform and the other in the train, Mr. Cluett yelled, "Wait a minute. I'm not going to camp!" He handed the rod to Bones and squeezed through the half-shut door.

"Whew!" Bones exhaled in relief, while the conductor looked annoyed and closed the door behind Mr. Cluett. Through the knapsack Bones felt for the oblong box Grandmother Twiggly had given him. "Sure couldn't eat fudge with Dad on the train!"

"You must starve at home," Whitey said sympathetically.

As the air conditioning became effective, the campers relaxed, chatted, or read comic books.

Bones glanced around the car. Every seat was occupied. "Are all these kids going to Crescendo?" he inquired.

"This is nothing," Whitey assured him. "More drive up, and some fly—from all over the country."

Whitey yanked his dungarees out of his knapsack and stood up.

With his dungarees rolled under his arm, Bones followed Whitey. His friend tripped over a leg in khaki trousers.

The owner of the leg, a sullen-looking boy who appeared older than most of the campers, glared at him through cold blue eyes and refused to withdraw his leg. "Fat and skinny," he taunted, pointing at Bones and Whitey. "Hey, Joe." He poked the boy next to him. "Look at this pair!"

While Bones watched Whitey's face grow red, he

clenched his fists trying to think of something appropriate
to say.

Joe had been talking with the girl behind him. He
glanced toward the boys, then at his friend. "Leave them
alone, Chester." He sounded annoyed at the interruption.

Each time Whitey tried to pass, Chester raised his leg.

"Maybe Chester would like a swat on his sunburned
nose," Bones offered at last. There was a trace of a grin
on his lips.

"Close your face," the big boy said, rising. He covered
Bones's cheek with an extended palm, then grabbed his
shirt. A button popped. "You're so fat you're busting your
clothes!"

By this time, campers were crowding around them.

"Relax," suggested Joe. "They're just kids."

Chester sat down. "Fat and skinny," he repeated as the boys walked by.

In the men's room, the boys changed their shorts for dungarees.

Whitey slapped his back pocket. "Ammunition," he said, taking out a box of raisins. He poured half the box into Bones's palm.

Bones pulled out a wad of bubble gum. "More ammunition." He opened the door of the men's room.

"Wait a minute," said Whitey, shutting the door. "This requires strategy."

Bones grimaced. "Yeah, he's bigger than we are."

"Exactly," agreed Whitey. "If he starts anything, we'll let him have it, and we'll be in the right."

Whitey was no fool, Bones realized. If a big fellow got rough, the rest of the kids would be on their side, but if they were the aggressors, the campers might look the other way. "I guess we should try to stay out of trouble," Bones admitted. He rolled the pink blob into a ball in the palm of his hand.

As Bones opened the door, a tall gangly boy about their age was waiting to get in. He waved a pair of dungarees at Whitey.

"Hi, Squid. Squid Wirtz, Bones Cluett." Whitey made the introductions. Pointing to the leggy boy with sparrow-colored hair and an undershot jaw, Whitey added, "He's a drummer. Man, does he move!"

Bones stared at Whitey in surprise. His friend never talked like this at home.

"See you guys." Squid waved his dungarees again.

The boys walked down the aisle, eyes straight ahead. This time they passed unnoticed. With our legs covered we blend in with the scenery, Bones decided. He reached for the unopened gift from Carolyn that he had left lying on his seat. "Guess we can eat the ammunition," he said, as he began to tear the black-and-gold wrapping off Carolyn's package.

"Better save it," suggested Whitey, who seemed familiar with the routine on the South Hill Special.

"We have better stuff to eat anyway," Bones said, remembering his grandmother's contribution. He crumpled the glossy paper into a ball and turned his new book over to read the title—*Sweet Substitutes*. "What kind of book is this?" He opened the book and glanced at the cover flap. " 'A is for apricot instead of almonds coated with chocolate, B is for bouillon, better than brioche.' " Bones turned to Whitey. "A dictionary for Martians?"

"Maybe it's a mistake," offered Whitey. "Maybe they wrapped the wrong book."

Bones continued reading. "Get a load of this. 'A firm *No* is more slimming than a three-mile hike. Eat to regain, not to regret, your figure.' " He turned to the title page. The words *Sweet Substitutes* were embellished with sketches of what his mother would call "wholesome fruits and vegetables." Then he picked up the small white card and turned it over. He read it and handed it to Whitey.

"Have a nice summer, Boney. Love, Carolyn."

"Some mistake," snorted Bones. "No wonder she said I should open it on the train." His jaw firmed as he announced, "I'll fix Carolyn. She wanted me to tack her snapshot above my bed so my counselor would write to her. I'll show her picture to the meanest guy in camp!"

"Chester!" Both boys whispered in unison. Bones's eyes danced with diabolical glee.

"But you can't just give it to him," Whitey stated thoughtfully.

"No, he'd suspect something," Bones agreed. "He's got to think he's taking something he's not supposed to have."

Bones chuckled. "I'll write her address on the back and just drop it at the right moment." He showed the snapshot to Whitey. "She almost looks good here."

Whitey studied Carolyn's picture. "Her dress is awfully short."

"That's a tennis outfit," Bones explained. "She doesn't know how to hold a racket, but she knows what to wear, and she takes two hours to primp for a game."

"Just like a girl," Whitey concluded.

Bones pulled a batch of comic books from his knapsack and stored his new book in their place. He slouched in his seat and commenced reading. When he looked up, he saw Squid, whose fingers curled around the suitcase rail, standing over them. Squid resembled a warped hammock billowing in the wind. Gripping the bar, he pushed out his torso, then retracted it. No wonder they called him Squid. He looked as if he were made out of jelly.

"You an acrobat or something?" Bones inquired.

"You should see him on the trampoline," said Whitey. "He can do a double back flip while he 'twists.'"

Bones snickered. "My family wanted to expose me to all the arts!"

"I'm starved," Squid declared. "Got anything good to eat?"

"Do I!" Bones shoved Carolyn's book to one side as he reached into the knapsack for Grandma Twiggly's fudge. He withdrew a shoe box secured with green-and-white string. Upon removing the lid, he found a note from Twiggs. "Have fun in camp, and don't eat all of this yourself!" He *must* be fat if she was getting after him!

"Any guys on the train from last year?" Whitey asked Squid.

Squid shook his head. His eyes lighted up when he saw the chunks of dark brown fudge. "This looks like the real stuff," he announced, squashing a crumb. He stuffed his mouth, then licked his fingers and rolled his eyes. "This is the same kind of chocolate they use in Wirtz Syrup, the 'Complete Syrup.' It must be the 'Complete Fudge,'" he jested.

"His father is the Wirtz Syrup King."

Bones looked impressed.

"Wait'll you taste Wirtz Syrup," Whitey continued exuberantly. "It's the gooiest!"

Squid was staring at the gear on the railing. "A geetar! Who plays?"

"Me," answered Bones. He swung down his instrument. "What do you like?"

"Me? Do you know that old funeral march?" Squid wiggled his shoulders. " 'Oh, when the saints, oh, when the saints . . .'"

"Got a dime, somebody? I lost my pick," declared Bones, looking around.

A girl in a striped skirt, sitting across the aisle, stuck out her loafer. "It's only a loan."

Bones pulled the coin out of the shoe.

Squid returned with his drums. Whitey unfastened his flute case.

" 'Oh, I want to be in that number, when the saints come marching in,'" a chorus of campers joined the instruments. The girl in the striped skirt acted as conductor.

Even Joe and Chester huddled over them. "Can you play 'The Boa Constrictor'?" Chester asked.

"I've heard of it," replied Bones, "but I haven't sounded it out yet."

Joe grabbed Bones's guitar. He accompanied himself, singing, " 'Slip right up, slither around. Be a boa constrictor . . .'"

While Joe was performing, Bones felt for Carolyn's picture in his pocket. He took it out and pretended to admire it. He waited for Chester's eye upon him before he let it drop, as if by accident. The snapshot landed under Squid's foot. Bones reached for it, letting Chester beat him by a fraction of a second.

"Give me that," Bones pleaded.

"Just a minute," said Chester.

"It's just my jerky sister," Bones stated.

"Sure, sure." Chester stared at the snapshot. "Maybe it is," he said at last. "She looks older than you. How old is she?"

"Seventeen," lied Bones.

"Think I'll keep this," announced Chester, sticking it into his breast pocket.

Bones tried to look angry. To stiffle a giggle, he cupped his hand over his mouth and stared out of the window at the cows, trees, and farms that resembled green patchwork quilts. He wondered how long it would take to get to South Hill, Vermont.

Whitey was nudging him. "We're going into the diner for a long Coke. We generally reach Albany around noon, and the dining car gets crowded. C'mon."

The dining car was practically empty and therefore cooler than the coach. "Let's stay here a long time," suggested Bones as he leaned back in his seat.

Whitey and Squid exchanged knowing smiles.

"Luncheon, boys?" the waiter asked hopefully as he passed out menus.

Bones opened the menu. " 'Lamb chops, three dollars'!" he exclaimed. "I'm not very hungry."

"Large Cokes for everybody?" Whitey inquired, looking around.

Squid and Bones assented with a nod.

"What's Crescendo like?" Bones asked, leaning on his

elbow and drumming a spoon against the white linen cloth. "What's it *really* like?"

Once again his two companions' eyes met.

"I told you about the activities," Whitey replied.

"I don't mean the activities. My family filled me in on that already. According to my parents, I'll be able to play every instrument in the orchestra when I come home, and Carolyn says I'll be so arty that I'll make mobiles by dangling hair rollers on twisted wire hangers." Bones became serious. "I mean what goes on in the cabins that isn't written in the catalogue?"

"Ho! Ho!" Squid laughed. "A lot depends on the counselors," he continued with a straight face. "But you'll survive."

3. The Bunk

Bones learned the first ritual of Camp Crescendo. One did not rush off the train, Whitey explained, because it was an advantage to be last. Then you would sit up front on the yellow buses that Bones could see from the train at the South Hill station.

"Those are the counselors." Whitey pointed to college-age boys in dark-green chinos and girls wearing shorts of the same color. They were checking lists, scratching their heads, and in some cases smiling. As a group, they did not look too stern, Bones decided.

"It's a little confusing at first," Squid remarked. "Nobody recognizes anyone else's real name. Everybody has a nickname here."

Bones stood on the seat to gather the gear from the rack. He handed the instruments and suitcases to Whitey. They slipped on their knapsacks, then politely waited for the train to clear. At last it was time to shuffle out.

"You look like a Christmas Eve shopper at Macy's!" exclaimed one of the counselors, grabbing the suitcase from Bones's left hand as he waddled down the train steps, his trombone tucked under his chin and his guitar in his right hand, which was also supporting the trombone.

"Thanks," said Bones when he reached the wooden platform.

"That's what I'm here for," replied the counselor, smiling. He was on the tall side, and Bones had to look up to meet his gaze. His eyes were an unusual color, Bones noted—gold with cocoa flecks in the sunlight.

"You might be one of my boys," the counselor continued, leading him toward the buses. "I'm Hank Fulweiler. What's your name?"

"Bones Cluett."

"Oh, yes." Hank appraised him from head to foot, then chuckled. "Had an interesting note from your father."

"Uh, oh." I'm cooked before I start, Bones thought. "Don't take my father too seriously," he pleaded.

"Why not?" Hank grinned, showing enamel-chipped square teeth. "He wants you to have plenty of exercise and a 'stick to your guns' diet. I was fat when I was your age," the counselor added matter of factly.

"You?" Bones asked incredulously. Hank looked like an advertisement for "Muscle Mike," the trimming studio in Shorehaven where all the fathers took steam baths and pedaled stationary bicycles. Mr. Cluett had taken him there once.

The bus held about thirty boys. Squid and Whitey occupied the second seat on the right in front. Bones and Hank sat ahead of them.

Whitey leaned over to read Hank's typewritten sheet. "Yowee! The three of us are together. Hey, Squid, Dick Bowman is in our cabin."

"Good thing," retorted Squid. "I'm not sure I brought my trunk key. Last year he opened my trunk with one of his screwdrivers."

"One of his screwdrivers? Sounds like a walking junk box!" exclaimed Bones.

"Nothing's safe with him around." Squid chuckled. "Remember those love letters last year?"

"Love letters," said Bones in disgust. "That's one thing I don't have to worry about."

"Don't be so sure," Hank teased. "There are girls at Camp Crescendo."

"And a camp postal system," Squid said helpfully.

"So you two are old campers." Hank had a genial manner, almost like an older brother. "You guys have to show me the ropes."

"We will." Squid rolled his eyes.

"Hm." Hank pursed his lips with a mock scowl.

The bus had been steadily climbing the graded dirt road. Grass had given way to a maple forest with leafy underbrush. The glare of the sun was dimmed by the trees, and the air was drier and cooler than it was at home.

Whitey tapped the window. "Raspberry bushes."

"Mixed with poison ivy," Squid cautioned.

The bus slowed down as the ascent grew steeper. A small mountain—or perhaps large stony hill—stood out in the distance.

"That's South Hill," explained Whitey. "It didn't quite grow into a mountain, but it's fun to climb it."

"Here we go." Squid stood up as the bus rolled between

two log pillars supporting a musical crescendo sign with *Camp Crescendo* written inside the emblem.

Bones realized that his expression must have registered disappointment, for Whitey said, "Nothing to see at the gate. This place is all spread out. Our cabins are near the boys' lake, and the girls' bunks are down that way." He pointed to a footpath on the right about fifty yards past the entrance. "Two hundred females live down there," he said, making a face. "We're outnumbered. There are only about a hundred and fifty boys here."

"We've got more muscle power," stated Squid, sitting down again as the bus rumbled over the bumpy road that was shaded by pine and maple trees.

"Main camp." Whitey tapped Bones's shoulder as they passed an area with a huge outdoor concert bowl, shingled cottages, and several oblong concrete buildings.

"Sit back," Hank ordered one smaller boy when they veered left and started down a sharp incline.

Bones saw what appeared to be a never-ending lake. Set back about twenty-five feet from its banks were log cabins, with pine trees shooting high above them.

As the boys jumped off the bus, a counselor assigned cabins.

"Is my trunk here?" Bones asked, following Hank.

"Oh, sure."

A boy with slicked-down red hair and large tan freckles opened the screen door of Cabin Eight and greeted the counselor.

As they entered, Hank said, "Boys, this is Charles Treehurst." Bones, Whitey, and Squid introduced themselves.

Then Whitey asked, "What do they call you for short? Leafy?"

"Charlie," the boy replied with the broad *a* accent of a Bostonian.

"Charlie, by Jove," mimicked Squid. As Bones moved over to his olive-green camp trunk tucked under the cot in a corner, he sensed that Charles Treehurst felt uncomfortable.

On the upper bunk bed across from him, a fellow was polishing a bugle. Whitey and Squid pulled the boy's leg. "Flip! Flip Hartig!" they shouted.

Flip jumped down and played the first bar of reveille. They laughed while another boy, small-framed and dark-haired, tossed a pillow at Bones.

"Tony Lamont," Flip said, introducing the boy. "He's an artist. Likes to draw cartoons."

"I'd better hide," Bones announced, nodding to Tony.

Hank pointed his finger at Flip. "You were right on the ball there with reveille. Time to make beds. If you guys are quick, we'll have a dip before supper."

Whitey hoisted his belongings onto the bunk above Bones. Squid captured the remaining upper bunk.

Bones searched his pockets for his trunk and duffel bag keys, then remembered they were in the shorts in his knapsack.

Squid kicked his trunk.

"There's one in every cabin," Whitey commented with a smirk in Squid's direction. "He never can find his keys."

Now Squid sat cross-legged on his upper cot, his chin resting on his fists, his eyes directed toward the ceiling.

With a swift gesture, Hank unloaded the contents of Squid's knapsack between the boy's legs. "You'd better clean house," the counselor ordered, fingering a crumpled bubble-gum wrapper, torn comics, bottle caps, and a long sticky caramel lollipop, wrapperless, that attached itself to the mattress.

Bones, who was anxious for a swim, remembered that when his mother could not find the key for his duffel bag, she had sent him down to the hardware store for another key and lock. He tossed his duffel bag key to Squid. "Try this. I think all these keys are the same. At least you may get your bedding."

"Who cares about blankets!" grumbled Squid. "I wanna go swimming, and my suit is in the trunk!"

"Octopus!" A voice boomed through the screen door.

"Genius!" Squid jumped to the planked floor and raced to open the door.

Bones saw a boy who was about his own height and had what Mr. Cluett would have called "consolidated" fat. He was weighted with a knapsack, a violin, and what looked like a plumber's tool kit. This must be Dick Bowman, Crescendo's self-appointed locksmith. Squid led him over to his trunk.

"Welcome aboard," Hank said to Dick. Then he introduced himself. Turning to Squid, the counselor motioned to the bed. "Clean it up! We'll have a 'white glove' inspection in fifteen minutes!"

Squid's jaw dropped while his eyes crossed. "A white—"

"Hospital corners." Hank pulled out the hastily tucked-in sides of the blankets on Bones's cot.

Bones repaired the damage without a word. At home his mother was so pleased when he made his bed that she never criticized, but here—well, things would be different.

The door opened again, and Bones imagined that things would not only be different, but that they would be difficult, for there in the doorway stood Chester—the boy with the cold blue eyes and black wavy hair, the boy who had baited them on the train and who now was in possession of Carolyn's picture. A camper stood beside Chester, and the camper looked like a miniature of the older boy.

"You must be the junior counselor." Hank extended his hand. "Welcome, J.C."

"Brilliant," Chester replied, ignoring Hank's gesture of friendship. With a smug, closed-lip smile, he introduced the boy at his side. "My cousin, Neil Palmer, the tennis champ of Craigsville, Pennsylvania." The junior counselor rubbed his fingernails on his shirt, stared at Bones, and continued, "The best athlete at Camp Crescendo, I venture, and he likes to box."

4. Uncle Willie

The short swim Hank had permitted them sharpened Bones's appetite. He wanted to snitch the last piece of fudge from his knapsack, but the counselor was on his heels.

"Get those wet suits on the line, boys," Hank ordered.

Chester handed his shiny blue trunks to Neil, just as the dinner bell clanged.

Hank looked critically at Bones. "Can't you do something with your hair?"

"What?" asked Bones, fingering the vertical strands. "Rubber cement?"

The counselor poured a colorless liquid onto Bones's scalp and massaged the boy's head hastily. "Comb it."

Bones did as he was told, then glanced at himself in the mirror. "It works."

"Sure," replied Hank, folding back Bones's collar and smiling.

Bones stared at Chester, who was running dental floss through his teeth and grinning at himself in the mirror. Hank caught Bones's eye and winked. His counselor had sized up Chester, Bones decided.

Before supper the boys had to line up for inspection, Boy Scout fashion. The tidiest cabin started the cafeteria line.

Tompkins, the head counselor, muttered to himself as he paced the row viewing the boys' palms. He sent several fellows back to wash more efficiently and let Cabin Four lead the contingent.

Bones was in Cabin Eight. Like the others he had to wait his turn on the cafeteria line. "Hamburgers, brownies, ice cream," the menu trickled down the line. Bones inhaled the fragrance of meat, and he pictured plump hamburgers crowned with crisp fried onions, a solid brownie, and two scoops of chocolate ice cream. At last he reached the metal trays, divided into five parts to accommodate the variety of items that made a supper at Camp Crescendo.

Bones thought he would sample everything.

"Two?" the boy behind the counter asked, clipping between tongs a flat slab of chopped meat about two and a half inches in diameter.

Bones nodded. Four would have been more like it.

"No rolls," Hank instructed the server when Bones waited for two hamburger rolls. "No potatoes." Hank continued down the line behind Bones.

Bones glared at his tray—two miniature hamburgers, a piece of lettuce adorned with a tomato sliver, a

shaky green gelatine square filled with random scraped carrots, and skim milk. No dessert at all—no brownie, no ice cream! How could they do this to him?

Cabin Eight had meals together. Bones listened to Hank say grace while his mouth watered as he glanced at the melting vanilla ice cream on all the other trays. He tried to imagine that he was eating Grandma Twiggly's fudge as his fork dipped into the gelatine.

During supper Hank briefed them on the evening camp meeting.

"It's the same every year," Dick Bowman announced unenthusiastically. "The faculty makes a little music, and Uncle Willie, the camp director, makes a speech. His favorite topic is 'Meat for the Soul, and Ice Cream for the Ego.'"

Bones scowled at Dick. He should have been tactful enough not to mention ice cream.

"What's an ego?" Bones asked when his tray was empty, and his lips had been licked for the last trace of food.

Dick shrugged his shoulders. "How should I know? But it sounds good." He looked inquiringly at Hank.

Bones observed that Chester offered no explanation. He was too busy wolfing down his brownie and stealing crumbs from his cousin Neil's tray.

Hank smiled. "I don't know whether I can explain this properly. The ego is sort of a personality manager. Your ego shows up in your dealings with other people. When you say a guy has a strong ego, you mean he's got confidence in himself. Sometimes you mean he's conceited."

Sounds like Chester, Bones reflected.

Hank paused to see if the boys were following him.

Chester stretched. "Don't you think these guys are a bit young for this conversation?"

Hank rubbed his forehead. "Maybe," he conceded,

"but they brought it up. Anyway, a fellow with a small ego doesn't think too much of himself. It's my guess that 'Ice Cream for the Ego' was the director's way of saying that by doing things you're good at, you strengthen your ego. You feel important."

"And 'Meat for the Soul'?" Bones pursued. He might as well get acquainted with this double talk.

Hank grinned at Bones. "That means working on the things that deserve work, even if they're no fun at first. Like sticking to your diet," he added, whispering into Bones's ear.

When everyone was through eating the boys rose to return their trays. Hank frowned as Chester handed his tray to Neil.

"OK, boys," Hank said, leading them out of the mess hall. "Let's finish unpacking and get the trunks on the rafters. Then you can do anything you want till camp meeting."

"Let's hurry, guys!" Squid shouted. "Then we can play soccer."

The boys stowed their belongings on battleship-gray shelves that lined the walls of the cabin. Bones lifted a pile of T-shirts, blushing at the sight of his name tag, Boniface Cluett. He unpacked quietly, not wishing to draw attention to what his parents considered "such a distinguished name."

Whitey seemed somewhat organized, and Leafy Treehurst was humming with contentment as he filled his shelves with wrinkle-free clothing, patting each stack gently to make room for more. Bones was relieved to see that Squid's shelves bulged even more than his own, and Squid's mood was one of resignation rather than pleasure.

Hank had unpacked before the boys arrived at camp. Now he supervised storage. He made Squid empty his shelves and begin over with even piles. He assigned space for toilet articles on the bathroom shelves, and both the counselor and the junior counselor hoisted trunks and duffel bags onto the rafters as they were emptied.

Tennis rackets, fishing rods, and musical instruments cluttered the aisles until the boys pushed their bulky things under the lower bunk beds—all but Squid's drums.

"I'll be able to leave these in the practice hall after classes start," Squid said apologetically. "Now can we play soccer?"

Hank shook his head. "Maybe tomorrow night. Camp meeting's in ten minutes."

At eight o'clock the whole camp filed through the gates of the outdoor stadium. Bones whistled along with the faculty orchestra's music. He recognized the melody— "When I Was a Lad," from *H.M.S. Pinafore.*

"The camp anthem," Whitey whispered as the boys followed the crowd down the dirt path that separated rows of brown benches.

Cabin Eight sat behind a group of younger boys. "They're juniors," Whitey stated in a superior voice.

Across the aisle, Bones observed girls wearing shorts and white shirts. Just like us, he mused, the uniforms did not make them look alike either. Some were pretty, and some were too fat. He wondered what they thought of him. Whitey must have read his thoughts for he said, "You'll meet the girls in your classes tomorrow."

Bones grimaced. His stomach began to somersault. It growled. He looked straight ahead, hoping to deter any glances that might come his way.

Now Willard Frenzl—Uncle Willie to the campers— was on the podium. "Welcome, campers, new friends and old friends," he began.

Bones tried to follow the speech, for he was impressed

with the soothing effect of the man's soft-spoken words. All human chatter had ceased. But the birds lacked reverence for the camp director, and their chirps harmonized with a bullfrog's croak. Bones glanced at Chester. The J.C.'s eyes were closed.

Uncle Willie was concluding now. Bones pinched himself to keep awake.

"We are here for your benefit—to help you become better musicians, better painters, better dancers, but most important, better people, better friends to one another. And I am confident that through your efforts Crescendo will increase in quality, for our hopes and our activities are the girders of a civilized society."

Bringing the heels of his palms together, Uncle Willie made a mock crescendo. It looked like a horizontal tent or a mountain that had toppled. The faculty orchestra closed the program with the anthem, while the camp director led the campers in the words:

When we were tots we knew that we would be
Climbers along the branches of the Crescendo tree,
Climbers along the branches of the Crescendo tree.
We paint so well. We toot so loud,
Our songs and dance make the whole world proud.

The jaunty tune and the enthusiasm of the campers around Bones lifted his spirits, making him anxious for the first day of classes. He inhaled the dry, pine-scented Vermont air, and knew that he would sleep well that night.

5. A Perfect *Bottom*

Bones soon discovered that Chester was a dandy. First, the J.C. acquired the nickname of Chesty when Tony Lamont caught him lifting dumbbells the following morning. Then, too, Chester's toilet kit was as elaborate as Carolyn's. Chesty was the only member of the cabin who used the mirror a lot, waxing his hairline, and smiling at himself while admiring his teeth.

Neil Palmer functioned robot style, performing for his cousin on demand. Neil never took the initiative, anticipated action, or uttered an original thought. If the boy liked to box, as Chester claimed, he failed to show it. Neil's tennis form, however, needed no correction. Hank Fulweiler was their tennis counselor, too, and Bones enjoyed watching him slaughter Neil on the courts, yet no intermediate boy could beat Chester's cousin or even come close.

After the first tennis lesson, Hank took Bones aside. "I want you to shellac this kid in the camp tournament."

"Me?" Bones knew he hit a tennis ball with good baseball form. He couldn't control his shots, and he rarely served the ball in the proper court.

Hank was smiling. "Tennis is more than hitting the ball. It requires strategy, outwitting the opponent. Seriously, tennis could do a lot for you."

"But what could I do for tennis?" Bones asked, patting his paunch.

"You could do something for me," Hank continued. "You could put Chester in his place. I hate to see Neil the goat, but maybe it would be good for him in the end." Hank shook his head. "The way that kid looks up to his smart aleck cousin! He ought to set his sights a little higher."

"Unless you can cook up some 'Instant Tennis,' there's not much hope for me," Bones protested. "What with dramatics, trombone class, the guitar band, swimming, and sailing, I'd have to learn to play tennis in my sleep!"

"I have some books," Hank said, "and there's a backboard behind the mess hall. I'll give you a couple of private lessons to get you started, and you'll have to go to the backboard every free minute you get."

Bones heaved a sigh. He could not picture himself competing against Neil in an exhibition match. He wasn't that interested in tennis, and he wasn't built for it.

Whitey, who had been acting as his personal camp guide, was waving to him now. "Hurry or we'll miss the bus," his friend called. Bones tucked his racket under his arm and ran.

Whitey was walking backwards, explaining, "Drama class is in main camp with the girls. It's a long hike if we miss the bus."

Bones huffed after Whitey. They didn't give a guy a free moment. From the time Flip Hartig had blown the ugly notes of reveille until this minute, Bones had been busy dressing, eating, cleaning the cabin, playing tennis —and now drama. Not seeing a bus, the boys walked the three-quarter-mile stretch to main camp where the coed classes and concerts were held.

"It's the Huber Building." Whitey began to run.

"Who's Huber?" Bones asked, breathing heavily.

"Oh, some rich guy who donated money to Camp Crescendo. The camp is always getting money to help young talent and all that jazz."

"You mean we're young talent?" Bones wondered what he was doing at Camp Crescendo. Too exhausted to run, he was trailing behind Whitey now.

Whitey stopped to wait. "It's the building between the trees." He pointed to a green shingled cottage that was perched on stilts to cope with the sloping ground.

When the boys entered the building, Bones was aware of girls' giggles and stares. One look at the drama teacher made him feel out of place. She was a gaunt-faced woman, her hair pulled together in one black pigtail, and her entire body save for her head and hands enveloped in one black leotard.

She turned her head toward the boys and the sides of her deep-red lips curled into a grin. With a wave in Bones's direction, she exclaimed, "A perfect *Bottom!*"

Bones's palms smacked the seat of his pants, while the class, which was three-quarters female, tittered appreciatively.

"You're right, Miss Granby." Good old Chesty was there to capitalize on Bones's distress.

"Find yourselves a place," the teacher said. She motioned toward an empty bench. "We're doing breathing exercises," she continued. "Ready now. Inhale for five counts, hold for five counts, and exhale saying *a-e-i-o-u*. Hold the *u* as long as you can." Her eyes scanned the room. "Chester, will you help that boy inhale." The teacher's arm extended toward Bones.

"With pleasure!" exclaimed Chester. With his palm he applied pressure to Bones's midriff.

Bones had difficulty holding his breath for those five long counts, but Chester would not let him exhale before they were over.

"Speak from your diaphragms, not from your throats," the woman directed, while the extended *u's* gradually diminished. "OK, everybody sit down," she said at last.

Next, scripts were passed down the rows of benches.

"We don't have a chance for a good part," Whitey explained. "The older kids get the breaks."

"That's good," replied Bones. "I think I'd like to sit and watch."

The play was *A Midsummer Night's Dream.* Bones glanced at the first page and then at Whitey. Whitey did not seem bothered by what he was reading.

"What language?" Bones inquired over Whitey's shoulder.

His friend laughed. "They do this one every year. This is one play where the orchestra and dance group can join in and perform, too. It ends up like a pageant, with everyone running around looking for a place to stand."

Miss Granby handed Bones a script. "Read over Bottom's part. I want you to try out for it."

So *Bottom* was a part after all! Bones and Whitey exchanged glances.

Chester was acting the big shot, going around listening to kids read parts and coaching them. He basked in the female admiration.

"What should I try out for?" Whitey wondered.

"You know this play better than I do," Bones reminded him.

Miss Granby relieved Whitey of further indecision. "I

fancy you'll make a tolerable Puck," she said to the tow-haired boy.

When the teacher had moved on, Bones mimicked her, "I fancy you'll make a tolerable Puck!"

"She always talks like that when we do Shakespeare," Whitey commented, "to set the mood. Wait till you see the get-ups—beards and purple stockings. Oh boy, are you gonna look cute!"

"I won't get a part," Bones said, although in a way he thought it might be fun.

Bones's cheeks reddened as he rose to read Bottom's part. " 'Mounsoo or,' " he began.

" 'M'sieu,' " corrected Miss Granby. "Start again."

" 'Mounsieur Cobweb; good mounsieur, get your weapons in your hand, and kill me a red-hipp'd humble-bee on the top of a thistle; and good mounsieur, bring me the money-bag.' "

" 'Honey-bag,' " Miss Granby interrupted.

This sounded silly, but Bones tried to read it with seriousness, if not with expression. He continued. " 'Do not fret yourself too much in the action, mounsieur, and, good mounsieur, have a care the honey-bag break not; I would be loath to have you overflown with a honey-bag, sig-ni-or.' "

" 'Seen-yore,' " the teacher said. "That's enough now. Your voice carries well." She nodded to Bones and said, "The makings of an ideal Bottom."

Again Bones winced. He might look the part, but that was all.

6. Two Knuckleheads

This time Bones and Whitey caught the bus. Bob Holburg, Cabin Four's counselor, drove them to the boys' side of camp.

"How is it you've got such clean guys in your cabin?" Bones asked Bob. "They always get to eat first."

" 'Cleffer's Magic Wall Wipe, guaranteed to clean anything—even hogs.' "

"Aw, they're all just sunburned and the dirt doesn't show," volunteered Dick Bowman, who was sitting a few rows behind Whitey and Bones. "I've got some paint remover. It ought to be as good as Wall Wipe. Aw," he remembered, "that stuff stings."

"You guys don't care about food anyway," Bob declared.

"Who doesn't care about food?" Bones folded his arms across the empty pit that was his stomach. "I'm the last in line. I get all the smells and nothing solid on my tray. That guy Hank poured skim milk on my protein cereal. It tasted like straw and water."

"I'll find a way to jimmy the deep freeze," Dick consoled him as the bus jerked to a stop a few yards from the square, low building made of cinder blocks where the boys ate. The fellows jumped off the bus and headed for their cabins. Bones heard shrieking and whistles from the lake.

When they entered the cabin, Squid dashed out of the door with his bathing trunks drooping below his navel, a towel and moccasins in his hands, and a sweatshirt between his teeth.

"You're losing something," Dick called.

Squid wiggled his torso. "No hips." His sweatshirt dropped out of his mouth. He picked up the shirt and tied it around his midriff.

"I wish I had his problems." Bones was thinking of his own apple-like knees and the fleshy roll above his waist. He never felt comfortable in a bathing suit unless he was in the water.

Discarded clothes lay strewn on the board floor. Leafy Treehurst struggled with the snapper of his rubber sandal. Tony attempted to take a knot out of the belt of his trunks with his teeth.

Dick opened his tool kit and tossed Tony a nail. "Try this."

"Somebody swiped my ear plugs," complained Whitey.

"We'll meet you down at the dock," Dick said to Whitey

as he pushed Bones toward the door. "Come on, man, run! We have to pass a thirty-minute swim test or be forever doomed to the crib."

"The crib?" Bones asked.

"The shallow roped-off area for nonswimmers," Dick explained.

The head swimming counselor blew a whistle. "Buddies line up."

Dick grabbed Bones by the hand.

"Everyone got a buddy?" the counselor continued. "When I blow the whistle, dive in, and see that you don't land on some guy's head!"

Whitey and Tony were running down the dock as the whistle blew. Leafy trotted behind them, flapping his sandals.

When all the boys were in the water, the instructor said, "Swim free-style out to the second float and back. Then remain in the water near me—treading, swimming, floating until I blow the whistle."

The water felt icy. Bones's skin tingled, and he began a vigorous crawl, not bothering to breathe until all his wind was gone. Then he turned over and eased into a lazy side stroke.

"Stay with your buddies," a counselor in a rowboat ordered.

Bones poked his head out of the water. Dick was about five feet ahead of him, doing a lusty breast stroke. Bones went back to the crawl, kicking hard to catch up with his buddy.

Suddenly Dick stopped, rolled over on his back, and began to float. Bones floated alongside of him. "You've got a powerful stroke there," Bones complimented him.

"Just keeping in practice," Dick replied. "I was the

champion free-style swimmer last year, and that took some doing, racing against Squid. He's halfway there when he dives into the water!"

The boys clustered near the dock. "How much time, Paul?" Squid asked the head swimming instructor.

"Nineteen minutes to go."

"What did he say?" inquired Whitey as he removed one ear plug.

"Nineteen," repeated Bones with exaggerated lip movements.

Squid pushed himself into the air, then closed his eyes and sank below the surface.

Bones trod water for a while, looking about him. This was boring. He did a dead man's float with his eyes open and watched tiny sunfish and minnows dart between the weeds of the clear water. The lake water didn't burn his eyes the way the water did when he swam in Long Island Sound, but it was more work staying afloat in fresh water.

A whistle blew. "Watch where you're going!"

Bones looked up in time to miss a leg of the dock.

"Move out," Paul ordered, gesturing away from the dock. "Five minutes more, frogs."

With only five minutes to go, the boys began to get playful. It was no longer necessary to conserve energy.

Bones dived beneath the water until he touched the muddy bottom with his fingers. Reversing the position, he balanced himself on a slimy stone. Then, closing his eyes, he propelled himself to the surface.

Crash! Bones felt an intense thwack against his crown. He must have blacked out, for the next thing he knew he was sitting on the edge of the dock with the head swimming counselor's hands supporting him under the

armpits. He shook his head and looked around. Dick
Bowman was beside him leaning against another instructor.

"Two knuckleheads!" Paul exclaimed.

Knuckleheads all right. Bones rubbed the swelling lump
on top of his head and glared at Dick.

"Don't give me the evil eye," declared Dick. "I was
sunning myself peacefully when a whale smashed into
me!"

Hank was down at the dock now, laughing with the
swimming counselors. "The two hardest heads in the division." Then soberly, he asked, "Do you think you can
walk, guys?"

The boys rose.

"What about the swimming tests?" Bones cried.

"Another time," Paul said.

"Oh, no," Bones groaned.

"It's all your fault," Dick grumbled. "Next time, look where you're going."

7. The Sick Boy

Rest period followed lunch. Bones found it impossible to lie still with an empty stomach. Whitey had promised to sneak him a roll, but when?

The boys lay on top of their blankets. The first half of rest period was designated as nap time. During the second half, they were allowed to write letters or read. Bones was formulating his message to his father. He would start by asking, "Why did you send me to camp? To lose weight or to have fun?"

Hank announced that he had to attend a meeting and was leaving Chesty in charge.

With the exception of Neil, the boys eyed the J.C. resentfully. He was reading a sports magazine. Soon, however, he let the magazine drop to the floor and wrapped the pillow around his head.

Bones stretched his head off the cot. His hands touched the bedding of the upper bunk. "The roll," he whispered to Whitey.

His friend put a crumbly muffin into his palm. Bones clutched it, crumbling it further, and deposited it under his pillow. As he sneaked pieces into his mouth, he became aware of Neil, watching him curiously from the adjacent lower cot, but the boy didn't say anything.

Soon Chester was snoring. First the boys signaled each other with their eyes, lest they disturb his slumber. When Chester, who had rolled over on his stomach, lay still for five minutes, Squid and Dick removed their shoes and tiptoed over to Bones and Whitey.

"Now's our chance," Dick began. "You name it. I'll do it."

"Get me a banana split," said Bones quickly.

"Be reasonable," Dick whispered. "I'm not a magician."

"We've got a case against Chester, haven't we, Bones?" Whitey asked.

"Careful," Bones cautioned. Neil was staring at them from the bunk across the way.

Dick stared bluntly back at Neil. "You a squealer?"

Neil shook his head.

"OK, turn over, then," Squid ordered. "If we get caught, we'll see that you don't get blamed."

Neil remained still.

"Turn over," Squid repeated.

"I just want to watch," Neil said. "I won't say anything, honest."

Evidently, Neil had only one captain. Well, Bones thought, after today, they'd know just how much of a stooge Neil really was.

Squid was staring up at the rafters. "You know that stuff he smears on his face after he shaves."

"You mean 'Conquistador, the Male Cologne,'" Bones said. There was a devilish expression on his face.

"Yeah!" Dick's eyes were gleaming. "A nice clear fluid. Just the color of turpentine." He raised his eyebrows and grinned. "I got the message!"

Bones surveyed Dick's equipment as he pulled out the can of turpentine. "White glue, too!" Bones almost shouted.

"Shush!" Whitey warned them. Chester had rolled over on his back, but his eyes remained shut.

Bones poked Dick and pointed to the glue. "For his roll-on deodorant," he explained softly.

"Umm," agreed Dick. "Goes well with toothpaste, too."

Bones grabbed Chester's aftershave lotion and deodorant, which were kept on a shelf under the mirror near the cabin door. He went into the bathroom for the toothpaste. Dick met him at the sink with glue and turpentine.

"Do you suppose we should throw this stuff into the toilet?" Bones asked in a whisper. He held up a square bottle of colorless fluid with a brass lid, then unscrewed the cap, and sniffed. Bones made a retching noise.

"Someone sick in there?" It was Hank's voice.

"I'll be all right." Bones tried to sound weak. That was a short meeting his counselor had attended.

"I'm holding his head," Dick announced casually and eased the door into a closed position.

"Whew!" Bones sighed. He dumped Chester's fancy solution into the toilet. The aroma of lilacs flooded the room. Quickly, Bones flushed the toilet.

"Feeling better?" Hank called to him.

"A little," Bones replied in a faltering voice.

"Need any help?" the counselor inquired.

"Patient's doing fine," Dick assured him, squeezing glue over the tip of the deodorant stick.

Bones turned on the faucet while he poured turpentine into the aftershave lotion bottle.

"Skip the toothpaste," murmured Dick, stashing everything in the shower.

"The smell!" The two boys said the words simultaneously.

"There's air freshener in the cabinet," Hank offered helpfully.

Bones and Dick bit their lips to keep from laughing.

When the boys opened the door to their bunk room, the other fellows were writing letters or reading comics.

Bones threw himself on his cot, face down, and remained still until the ringing of the bell that signaled the end of rest hour.

When he turned over, Hank was standing above him. "Didn't think you had enough in your stomach to throw up. Want to rest this afternoon?" the counselor asked in a tone of sympathy.

Bones smiled weakly. "I'm OK. Anyway, I'll be sitting down most of the afternoon. Trombone and guitar classes," he explained.

"All right," said Hank, "but if you change your mind, just come on back."

To Bones's and Dick's relief, Chester was the first one out the door. When Hank left the cabin, Dick retrieved his turpentine and glue, and Whitey waited while Bones put back Chester's toilet articles. Their tasks made them miss the bus to main camp.

"It's too hot to hurry," Bones announced. His guitar was strapped across his shoulder, and he held the handle of his trombone case.

"I have orchestra," Dick said, running ahead. "I want to try out for concert master," he declared, waving his violin case in the air.

"You're not the type," Bones called as he watched his friend race forward.

"I gotta go, too," said Whitey. Whitey played the flute in the orchestra.

"But how do I find the guitar class?" Bones asked. "I'll get lost."

"It's right near the outdoor bowl. Ask anyone."

"Where's the outdoor bowl?"

"You were there last night," Whitey reminded him. "Just keep walking straight."

Now Bones was on his own. He did not rush, and when he arrived at main camp, the area was deserted. There was the bowl and beside it a brown wooden building. Bones ambled up the steps, listening to waltzy piano music. This didn't sound right, but he opened the screen door anyway.

"*Demi-plié,* now stretch." An instructor wearing pink-knitted leg warmers over dancing tights gave the orders.

Girls in leotards were lined up against the walls. Their right arms clung to the bar. Heels together, they made a half-squat, then thrust their heads and left arms backward.

With his hand on the doorknob, Bones remained motionless, his mouth agape, as he realized that he had just walked into a girls' ballet class. Before he could back out unnoticed, the music stopped, and the girls began to laugh. The teacher turned around, and Bones was caught, speechless with chagrin. "Well? What do *you* want?" she asked.

"I—I guess I came to the wrong place," he stammered awkwardly.

"You can join us if you like," the teacher said with a twinkle in her gray eyes. "What are you looking for?"

"The guitar class."

"I know where that is. I'll show him," one of the girls offered.

"What's your name?" the pixie-faced ballerina asked as they descended the steps.

"Bones Cluett."

"Bones!" she exclaimed. "Meatball is more like it! That's what I'll call you."

If I can help it, you'll never see me again, Bones

thought. But not to seem rude, he asked, "What do they call you?"

"Prue," she said coyly. "My real name is Prunella. Prunella Boggs."

That's a mouthful, Bones was thinking. Out loud, he commented, "Pruneface and meatball. We'll make a delicious combination."

Prue stuck her tongue out at him. "Next time I won't volunteer to help a stray wolf."

"You've got me wrong, Pruneface. I'm just a mislaid meatball."

"I won't forget it!" the girl declared, pointing to a stucco building. "It's in the basement," she said and dashed back to class.

Bones discovered that his tardiness was unimportant today for each class member had to play a solo, and several had not yet performed. Although he recognized some of the faces of the boys from the intermediate division, the class was filled with fellows and girls he had never met.

Bones noted that the instructor looked as old as his father, yet wore the counselor's uniform—dark green chinos and a white, short-sleeved shirt. The teacher did not interrupt the class to acknowledge Bones's presence. "Next," he said.

A short girl with what Carolyn called a "teased" hair-do rose. Her coiffure must have added at least three inches to her height, Bones decided, as she announced her selection. "I'll play 'Für Elise,'" she said.

"Beethoven." The man nodded his approval. "Your name?"

"Millicent, Millie Kuhn," the girl answered, smoothing the dark nest above her forehead.

Bones listened to the trilly waltz music with increasing

discomfort. He was beginning to feel that no class would be any fun. Oh, for a rugged game of baseball!

He wondered what he should play as the others performed. He heard "Humoresque," "Minuet in G," and the "Habanera" from *Carmen*. Finally, one of the boys had the courage to play a folk song, and Bones relaxed a little.

"As I said earlier, my name is Forster. You, young man," the teacher was talking to Bones now. "Will you introduce yourself to the class?"

"Bones, Bones Cluett." Bones remained seated as he spoke and looked straight ahead. "I'll play the 'Austrian Hymn.'" That was by Haydn, and it was the only classical music he knew.

Listening to himself, Bones realized that he sounded mechanical. His fingers felt stiff before so many strangers.

When his solo was completed, Forster looked at him without smiling. "Now play us something you like."

"You mean it?" Bones asked with a grin. He did not wait for a reply, but letting his wrist relax, he strummed the beginning bars of his favorite song, "The Tuckered Pretzel."

The "twist" rhythm inspired rotating shoulders and waving arms. "'The Boa Constrictor,'" the students shouted, before the instructor had a chance to intervene. As Bones's pick hit the strings, the kids sang:

> *Slip right up, slither around.*
> *Be a boa constrictor. Be a mound.*
> *Need no drape. Need no shape.*
> *Just open up wide, and swallow an ape.*

When the song was over, Forster exclaimed, "That's a beatnik ditty if I ever heard one. Where did you pick it up?"

"On the train," Bones replied. "Everyone knows it."

"So I see!" Forster declared. "What else do you kids know?"

That remark was the signal for a jam session. Calypso, rock'n'roll, and jazz followed. Feet stamped against the floor while the picks plucked the strings.

Forster consulted his watch. "End of the period."

The youngsters continued to play the remaining bars of "Bill Bailey, Won't You Please Come Home."

Elated by his guitar class, Bones realized that this must be what Hank meant when he had described "Ice Cream for the Ego." This was easy, this was fun, and, in a way, it made him feel important.

His buoyant spirits dropped as soon as he entered the cottage where the dreaded trombone class met. Now Bones could feel a weight in the pit of his stomach. Again, he saw rows of chairs. Bones selected the last seat in the middle row. No matter which way they started, he would not be first.

As the seats were occupied, Bones observed that save for two girls, taller and older-looking than himself, this would be a male class. Fellows around him were testing their trombones. They didn't sound like beginners. He wondered if he was in the wrong class.

A bald-headed man, who looked even older than Forster, entered the cottage. His neck was engraved with ridges, and Bones saw gold caps on his front teeth as he walked around the room, smiling and greeting the ones he knew.

The man stood in front of the class now, waiting for the murmuring to cease. Reluctantly, Bones removed his instrument from its case.

The instructor said, "For those of you who don't know

me, the name is Pierce. Rhymes with fierce," he added, narrowing his dark eyes into a make-believe scowl. "If you just say your name and play the C scale, I'll get to know you."

You sure will, Bones thought, for never in his entire life had he blown a full note on the trombone. If he learned to play the scale by the end of the summer, he would consider it an accomplishment.

"You look as if you've got plenty of wind," Pierce declared when it was Bones's turn.

Rather than explain that he was a genuine beginner, Bones demonstrated. His forehead wrinkled and his face crimsoned out to his ears as he tried to blow all his breath into the mouthpiece.

"Don't play with your eyebrows. Play with your lips," Pierce ordered as the vibrations of a deflating balloon came from Bones's horn.

"Sing that note."

Bones hummed middle C.

"Now make your horn sing."

The Bronx cheer emanated from his trombone.

"I don't know what I'm doing," Bones said breathlessly. "I've never played the trombone before."

"I believe you," the instructor conceded. "You'll need a little extra help. You've got to learn to control your lips."

After the others had performed, Mr. Pierce went up to Bones. He picked up his trombone. "A fine instrument."

"It was my father's," Bones acknowledged, wishing his father were here in his place.

"You take your chair, and I'll carry the trombone," the teacher said. "We'll let you practice in the woods. I'll be right back," he told the class as he and Bones went outdoors. Pierce paused about twenty feet from the cottage under a maple tree. A little screening, Bones noted with relief, observing that he was within view of the Huber Building.

Mr. Pierce showed him how to hold the trombone and how to use the slide to achieve different notes. "Just get acquainted with the instrument today, and experiment with the sounds as you change your lip positions. Remember, the tighter the lip, the higher the pitch," he explained and then left before Bones had a chance to try.

Bones waited until his instructor had entered the cottage before putting his lips to the mouthpiece. His cheeks were puffed out, and he expected to explode a mighty blast when he saw Chester and a man dressed in city clothes walk out of the rear door of the Huber Building.

Bones put down his horn and waited, hoping they would walk away, but they sat down on the wooden steps, facing him.

He would not give Chester anything more to tease him about. It was bad enough being called "Fatty" by that conceited jerk. Bones worked the slide back and forth and polished the brass against his shorts. So far he was certain he had not been observed, for the two appeared to be engrossed in conversation.

Suddenly, Chester stood up and turned to the man. "I can't!" he protested loudly.

The man turned his head furtively in all directions, then pulled at Chester's sleeve. The J.C. sat down. They continued their conversation in low tones until Chester stood up again. He started up the steps, looking back at his companion, who remained on the bottom stair.

Chester put his hand on the doorknob and shook his head. "It'll never work, but I'll try."

"It better work," the man said gruffly and walked away.

What better work? Bones pondered. He lifted the trombone to his lips. When he was sure no one was in sight, he pushed out the slide and blew into his horn. A note sounded. More like a fog warning than music, but it was the least painful noise that had come out of his trombone so far!

8. The Volunteer Female Fire Brigade

After twenty minutes of tussling with the trombone, Bones's lips began to feel sore and puffy. Happily, he saw the kids come out of the cottage, and he returned to retrieve his case. At the doorway he met Pierce.

"I was just coming out to see how you were doing."

Bones shook his head. "I'll never learn the scale."

"Have you got a minute? I'd like to hear you again."

Bones obliged by blowing a few foghorn warnings.

"It's coming. It's coming," the instructor said kindly. "Try once more, and take it slower. Gradually, push the air into your *horn* instead of puffing your cheeks."

Bones made a few more attempts until one clear toot sounded.

"There!" Pierce shouted. "Practice in your free time."

What free time? Bones wanted to say. He was thinking of all the things that were piling up—practicing at the backboard, for example, and studying the stupid script that he couldn't even read correctly, much less understand. Wasn't there any time for fun?

"Don't forget your guitar," the instructor called to him as he started to leave.

"Thanks." Bones pulled the guitar strap over his shoulder. As an afterthought he said, "Don't know where I can practice. The kids in the cabin won't appreciate my music."

"There's always the woods," Pierce reminded him.

There's always the woods, Bones said to himself as he walked toward the bus stop. Then he grinned, imagining Chester sprucing up for the evening activities.

"Just my luck!" Bones groaned when he saw the bus rolling down the path, beyond shouting distance.

The guitar strap rubbed against the side of his neck. He put down the trombone to switch the guitar to his other shoulder. Then he saw that the bus had stopped. Maybe one of the kids had seen him.

That was funny—all the boys were piling out of the bus. Bob Holburg was motioning the fellows away from the vehicle. Perhaps there had been too much horseplay, and he was going to make them walk. Bones began to run. The guitar bounced against his side.

As he drew near, he saw smoke coming out of the driver's window, and he smelled rubber burning.

"Keep away!" Bob shrieked. "Get over with the other guys!"

"Aren't you going to put it out?"

"Sure," Bob answered, "but the safety of the campers is my first consideration."

"Should I go back to main camp for water?" Bones wondered how the fire had started.

"No, wait!" The counselor pointed to a path a few feet ahead of the smoldering bus. He tossed Bones his whistle. "Down there's the intermediate girls' division. Blow before you enter! And tell them to round up water in anything! Even their shoes!" he shouted.

Bones dropped his instruments and ran. He blew the whistle where the path ended and the girls' campsite began. "Ahoy, there!" he called. His voice cracked, but he didn't sound like a girl.

Heads, some teased like angry mops, some crowned with dripping stringy locks, others with rollers bobbing, popped out of doorways. Girls sped toward him.

"Out of bounds, young man." Bones felt two hands press against his shoulders and twist him around.

He faced a counselor nearly six feet tall, wearing a towel sarong-fashion.

"There's a fire!" he yelled.

"Why didn't you say so?"

He was obviously more embarrassed than she. "We need all the water we can get. The bus is on fire!"

"Fill your trash cans with water, girls, and fill everything else that's available!" the counselor ordered. "This young man will lead the way."

A volunteer female fire brigade! Serious as the situation was, Bones found himself snickering while the group assembled. They ran with water splashing from scalloped bathing caps, plastic bags, and waste cans. Some even carried glasses of water.

"Hi, Meatball!"

"Oh, no!" Bones grimaced. With straight hair pressed flat against her head, the ballerina Pruneface leaped toward him. She wore a two-piece yellow bathing suit and

spilled water from two glasses as she raced to reach him first.

Bones turned around and fled toward the burning bus. "Hurry," he commanded, letting the girls struggle with their loads of water.

Bob Holburg met him along the path. "Some gentleman!" The counselor ran past Bones and grabbed a pink trash can. Bones followed his example.

The girls ran to the bus and flooded the driver's seat.

"I'll have to wear a bathing suit to drive this thing," Bob announced. "That's enough water or we'll have to use a paddle."

The fire had been a minor one. The seat was charred, part of the rubber mat below the seat had simmered and still reeked, but the smoke was gone.

"Much obliged, girls," Bob said gallantly.

The fire brigade waved good-by.

Prue screeched, "So long, Meatball!"

"Who's Meatball?" the other guys asked.

Bones's blush gave away his new title. I'll fix her, he thought, listening to high-pitched male voices echo the unwanted nickname.

"Shut up! Next time one of you guys can run through enemy territory."

Gradually the boys settled down and began to return to the bus. Bones stepped up front to Bob. "How did the fire start?"

The counselor's face clouded. He spoke slowly. "It was a moderate fire, the kind that could have been caused by a cigarette butt." He paused and then added, "Only, I don't smoke."

"It's a good thing," Bones commented.

"Yeah, I could get into a lot of trouble." Bob shook his

head. "I may anyway. I'm the only one who drives this buggy. Beats me how this thing started."

"Do you suppose we'll ever find out?"

Bob shrugged his shoulders.

9. Temper, Temper

Leafy Treehurst was applying calamine lotion to his ankles when Bones returned to his cabin after the free swim period.

"Those insects are carnivorous!" Leafy exclaimed.

"Then they had no business attacking a plant like you," Bones teased.

"Oh, they won't again," Leafy replied in a determined voice. Methodically, he began to spray insect repellent on the unclothed areas of his body.

"I'm allergic to bites," Leafy explained.

"Who isn't?" piped up Tony. "Got some extra calamine? I think I picked up poison ivy this afternoon when we were painting in the woods."

Leafy walked toward him with the white solution and a blob of cotton. Tony turned around and pointed. "Behind the knees."

Bones was examining Treehurst's medicine kit. "You sure came prepared. You use all this stuff?" He picked up a bottle of nose drops.

"I'm hyperallergic," Leafy stated matter-of-factly. "It's a nuisance sometimes."

"You're what?" asked Bones.

"Things bother him," Whitey translated. "Some things make him sneeze; others make him itch."

"Man, you got troubles," Squid said to Leafy, swatting his towel in Neil's direction.

"Lay off," Bones said to Squid. "Neil's got troubles, too."

"I know what you mean." Squid walked over to Neil. "You say anything to Chester?"

Neil shook his head.

Bones was beginning to feel sorry for Neil. Being related to a J.C. set him apart from his cabinmates, and Chester seemed to encourage the breach. Neil seemed painfully shy and he rarely spoke. Bones waved his comics at the boy. "I'm finished with these if you want to borrow them."

"Thanks." Neil flashed an unexpected smile.

Flip Hartig, the bugler, said, "I've got a knapsack full of comics if anyone wants them."

"We'd better hide them," cautioned Squid. "Maybe Hank doesn't know it, but Crescendo campers are supposed to read the *Opera News* instead of *The Magnetic Fleas* or *The Mystery of the Lazy Leech*."

"Yeah, they're supposed to confiscate comics," Flip remembered, "to encourage growth in reading. My mom packed a bunch of highbrow books to give the right impression, or maybe she thinks I'll be desperate enough to read *A Tale of Two Cities*."

"That's a good book," Leafy said, "once you get into it."

"Who's got time to get into it?" Squid asked, executing a backbend over Dick's cot.

Chesty and Hank came back from their swim.

"Heard you two knuckleheads passed the swim test this afternoon," their counselor remarked.

Dick and Bones eyed one another, grinned, and nodded.

Chester became attentive. "Knucklehead?" He eyed Bones. "Fatty has *another* nickname. *Bottom,* the perfect *Bottom!* Miss Granby thinks he can act. I don't think he can even read Shakespeare!"

"Did you at his age?"

Chester might be his enemy, Bones thought, but Hank was his friend. He gave the counselor a grateful smile.

The J.C. did not offer a reply. He tossed his wet suit at Neil, grabbed his shaving gear and towel, and strode into the bathroom.

"Let's see how clean you mud pies can look. I'm hungry tonight," Hank declared, "and I want to be first in the chow line."

"You don't even know what hunger is!" exclaimed Bones.

"There, there," Hank said, patting the top of Bones's head. "Your stomach will shrink pretty soon, and you won't even want to eat."

"How much do you want to bet?"

"A chocolate malt? In a week?"

"I may evaporate in a week," said Bones.

Chesty came out of the bathroom. It was Hank's turn.

The J.C. walked up to the mirror, examined a razor cut on his chin, and blotted his face with a tissue.

Dick stood in a corner studying his violin music. "Bum de bum, bum bum," he chanted and moved his arm in rhythm.

Bones picked up his script, marveling at his cohort's nonchalance.

Chesty smiled at himself in the mirror and reached for the bottle of Conquistador. He poured a generous supply of the liquid into his palms, closed his eyes, and smeared his face. "Ow!" The J.C. gasped. "It stings!" He smelled his hand. "Turpentine!" he shrieked.

Chester wheeled around. He began to pace the cabin. "So you little pipsqueaks wanna play tricks!" He stared at each one of them in turn until his eyes rested on Bones. "I suppose it was you! You little dough-faced snake!"

"Don't blame him! It was all of us!" the others cried in unison.

Wide-eyed, Chester stared in disbelief at Neil. "You knew about this? You let them do this to me?"

Hank, freshly shaven, walked back into the room.

"How about a little lotion?" Chester asked. Gallantly, he offered the counselor the uncapped bottle of Conquistador.

The boys stood with their mouths open until Hank said, "No thanks. H_2O is good enough for me."

"Smell this," persisted Chester.

"I know it's great stuff," Hank conceded.

"Go on, smell it." Chester held the bottle under Hank's nose.

"Man, you got gypped! That's turpentine!"

With a diabolical laugh, Chester said, "I got gypped all right, by your little angel faces. My own cousin Neil was corrupted by these hoods!"

Hank scratched his head. Then he turned to Neil and grinned. "You too?" he asked.

The counselor's grin was contagious. Neil ventured a small smile.

At this point, Hank endeavored to scowl. He tapped his lips with his index finger and glanced around the cabin. "OK, fellas, you had your little joke. Now give Chester back his aftershave lotion. Where did you put it?"

Dick and Bones looked panic-stricken.

"Come on," said Hank. "Give it back. It's expensive stuff."

"Five dollars a bottle," Chester informed them.

"We can't give it back," Bones said sheepishly. "I flushed it down the toilet."

Hank was having difficulty keeping a straight face, but Bones could see that he was determined to be fair to Chester.

"I'll pay for it," said Bones.

"We were all in on this," Flip announced. The others echoed his statement.

"You boys are all right." Hank's face registered approval. He turned to Chester. "Don't get me wrong. I'm not in favor of these practical jokes, but at least we have unity in our cabin."

"Yeah." The J.C. uttered a hollow laugh. "They're all united against Chester."

"Wars," Leafy said quickly, "always bring out the best in men."

"A profound statement, Treehurst." There was a twinkle in Hank's eyes, but no trace of a smile on his lips. "Now we need a peace treaty." He looked at the boys. "How much do they give you kids to spend? Thirty cents a week, I believe."

"Yeah. We get ten cents three days a week to buy ice cream or candy at the canteen," Dick volunteered. His voice carried resentment.

Hank turned to Chester. "That's not so bad. You'll be squared away in a little over two weeks."

"What am I supposed to do in the meantime?" Chester asked, picking up his roll-on deodorant.

Bones held his breath while the J.C. applied the stick, but there was no reaction from Chester.

Hank meditated.

Bones and Dick chewed their fingernails to restrain their amusement. Evidently the glue had dried, and the J.C. didn't know the difference.

"Tell you what," Hank said at last. "I'll give you the five dollars and the boys can pay me back."

The junior counselor looked at Hank suspiciously. "You're awfully obliging. Were you in on this, too?"

Hank laughed and shook his head. "No, I wasn't in on this. I can't condone this sort of thing. You should know that. But," he added, "I was a kid once. Kids like to set off fireworks, and they don't mind getting into trouble if the reaction is worth it."

Chester looked at the faces around him.

Bones draped his arm across Neil's shoulder. Squid was standing on one foot, rotating his other ankle in the air. The rest of the boys busied themselves putting away towels, comics, and instruments.

At last, Chester said, "Well, boys, was it a good reaction?"

Still not sure of the J.C., the fellows chuckled half-heartedly.

"C'mon boys," Chester persisted. "At least you can say I'm a good actor."

Bones's eyes leveled with Chester's. "If that was acting, you deserve an 'Oscar'!"

10. The Angle of Reflection

The first week of camp was a matter of adjusting to the routine. Things worked out as Bones had predicted. Guitar class was fun. Learning the trombone was a chore, and Bones continued to feel out of his element in drama. However, Miss Granby was determined to make him into a first class Bottom.

As for the sports, swimming and sailing were pure relaxation, but not tennis! Hank was a martinet on the courts. The counselor had been serious about shaping him into a tennis champ.

"Run. Straighten your arm. Change your grip. Keep your eye on the ball. You're playing tennis, not baseball." Bones went to sleep at night with Hank hounding him in

his dreams, but he was beginning to analyze his own game, and he often anticipated Hank's phrases.

Near the end of the second week at Crescendo, the counselor was watching him at the backboard.

Bones hit a high, wild ball. "I know. I didn't put my side to the net."

Hank nodded approvingly. "You don't need me any more. You know all your faults."

"That's not gonna make me win a tennis match, and you know it!"

"To tell you the truth," Hank began, "I not only don't care whether or not you win, but I almost don't want you to. I'll feel sorry for Neil."

Bones knew what was in Hank's mind. Neil lost all his self-consciousness while playing tennis or rehashing his game afterward. A defeat on the courts, as if such a thing were possible, would push him back into the shell he was gradually leaving.

"Then what are you bugging me for, anyway?" Bones asked.

"It's become a habit," Hank explained. "In the beginning when Chester boasted that his cousin could win any match hands down, I wanted to cook up a little competition for Neil."

"I think I get it," Bones replied. "Neil doesn't hang up his cousin's suit any more or empty his tray." Moreover, Bones reflected, the two boys seemed to be separated by their interests. Chester practically inhabited the Huber Building these days, while Neil was drawn to the red clay courts. "Neil is different now," Bones declared thoughtfully.

"Exactly," said Hank. "Neil has discovered it's more fun to be one of the boys than to be Chester's lackey. Chester has lost interest in his young cousin."

"So who are we fighting?"

"We're not fighting anyone." Hank grinned broadly. "You probably think I'm nuts for pushing you anyway, but you were a natural for me to pick. I spotted you as a smart kid, and your father wanted you to get a workout."

"Yes, but my father never said I had to become a tennis pro. He'd be satisfied if you just starved me."

"You lose weight quicker if you burn up energy," Hank argued, "and I decided to transform you into an ace in the process." The counselor was smiling now. "Of course, I anticipated a little reflected glory for my efforts."

"You schemer," said Bones. "No wonder you watch my diet like a horse trainer."

"Yep. Your father is in for a surprise. He's going to find a skinny Bones."

"Things are getting loose," Bones admitted. "I'm having trouble keeping my pants up."

"Move the button."

Bones's eyes popped. "Me?"

"Well, then," Hank suggested, "get one of your girl friends to do it. You know the one who calls you 'Meatball'—she's got a soft spot for you. She's kinda cute, too," the counselor teased.

"Pruneface cute?" Bones pretended to retch. "She walks around real snobbish-like—her head up and her hair combed."

"You'll change," the counselor said, whacking Bones's rump with his racket. He motioned toward the backboard. "Enough stalling. I'm going to show you one more thing— then you're on your own. It's called the angle of reflection."

"The huh? Speak English," Bones pleaded.

"I'll demonstrate." The counselor moved to the far right of the backboard court, then thwacked the ball with his racket. It hit the center of the backboard and bounced at an obtuse angle onto the left side of the macadam. "Get it? The angle at which you hit the ball is the angle that it will return to you on the opposite side."

"Yes, but this is a backboard. When you play against a person that doesn't happen," Bones protested.

"Not if they can direct the ball," Hank admitted. "But if you hit a hard ball, and your opponent's racket head is parallel to the net, one little tap will send it in the opposite direction from where you were."

"If he doesn't follow through," Bones added smugly.

Hank laughed. "You've got the lingo. Actually he can follow through and direct it to the other side, too. But the point is that the defensive player generally doesn't have time to follow through. All he hopes to do is get it back and work himself into a better position."

"But you told me to aim for the corners, to keep the guy running."

"Sure," the counselor agreed. "But be prepared when the angle of reflection rebounds on you. Incidentally, it's a beautiful net play. The ball hits a straight racket and bounces to the opposite side, just the way it did on the backboard."

"Pretty tricky," Bones conceded.

Hank tossed the balls into the can and looked at Bones. "If words could win, you'd walk away with the match." He cocked his head to one side, and with his fist, he made a mock jab at Bones's jaw. "With lots of practice, you have a fighting chance."

11. Good-by, Sweet Syrup

After lunch on the fourth Monday of camp, Bones's stomach was full of skim milk, but his mouth was aching for a piece of fudge.

The mail added to his frustration. Just looking at Midge's scrawl made him hungry. He could visualize her climbing on top of the refrigerator to the cookie cabinet, choosing among the goodies available—Twigg's home-made brownies, store-bought chocolate puffs filled with marshmallow and raspberry jelly. Even a graham cracker would be welcome to Bones at the moment.

He could almost smell the buttery dough baking as he read:

Dear Boney,

Grandma and I are baking your faverit choklet pretsils. But we cant send you some tho cause your on a diet.

Daddy says you shud look grate by end of sumer. Momy says you will be a skelatin. Dont they feed you at camp? I miss you very much.

Love your sister Midge.

P.S. Grandma would sent you comics, but Momy says they are not aloud at camp crashendo. Carolyn got a letter and pickture from your conselor. I read it. He looks very pretty.

Bones roared and showed his sister's letter to Whitey. "Chester would appreciate that," he whispered, pointing to the last sentence.

The junior counselor was engrossed in his own mail, and though Carolyn hadn't even mentioned Chester in her letter to Bones, he was almost positive he recognized her handwriting. He felt a twinge of guilt at the thought of his sister corresponding with the cocky J.C. Serves her right, he reassured himself, for wasting her money on that book, *Sweet Substitutes*. There was *no* substitute for sweets!

"We need a couple of strong men," Hank announced, flexing his muscles. "We've got some heavy packages to carry."

"Yahoo!" Dick squealed. With him, Squid, Whitey, and Flip leaped off their cots. "The *Worst* syrup is here!"

"*We'll* help!" The boys ran out of the door ahead of their counselor.

When Hank and the boys returned with the bundles, Squid announced proudly, "A case for each guy in the cabin! My dad does this every year."

"He promotes the chocolate habit," Leafy remarked. "He's no fool."

Flip licked his lips. "Takes the monotony out of camp cooking. Wait till you try it, fellas!"

"Can we sample it now?" Tony asked, rubbing his palms.

"Hold on, boys," cautioned Hank. "You can each take a can up to the mess hall."

"Me too?" Bones asked, reading the label on one of the cartons, *Wirtz Syrup Manufacturing Co.*

"I'll have to confiscate yours," Hank informed Bones apologetically.

"You might as well send it home to my kid sister." Bones could not get himself to pronounce the word "syrup." He had promised Midge a surprise anyway, a gift from camp, when she cried at the station. A case of Wirtz Syrup ought to be more exciting than a stuffed animal purchased at the camp store. Still, you never could tell. Girls had funny ideas.

Bones stood aloof now as the boys tore open the boxes. Tony jumped for joy. "Your dad sure is generous."

A glimpse of the brown-and-gold label set Bones day-dreaming. He visualized a glacier of vanilla ice cream speckled with ground vanilla bean. He could see chocolate lava, Wirtz Syrup, oozing down and thickening against the slopes of this thawing mountain.

"It's like being tickled to death!" Bones wailed.

"I'll see that your sister gets it," the counselor said kindly. He started back with the empty cartons mounted on his shoulder as the boys stored the cases under the lower bunks.

"You mean I have to live with this stuff?" Bones covered his eyes.

While Chester was engaged in waxing his front hairline,

Dick walked over to Bones. "I've got a screwdriver and a hammer. I'll open a can in the cabin for you later on."

"Whatcha sprucing up for, Chesty?" Squid grabbed the J.C.'s dumbbells. "Dontcha know it's rest hour?"

"Put those down," Chester demanded. "You might kill someone with those things."

"I just want to get muscles like yours." Squid continued to hold the dumbbells, expanding his chest and extending his arms. The weights wobbled in his hands. "Ow! That hurts!" he squawked.

"Cut it out!" Chester grabbed the weights. "This takes a strong guy."

"Let me try it," Bones said. He lifted the dumbbells, in imitation of Chester. His arms hurt, but he camouflaged the pain with a grin.

Chester was staring at him. "That's pretty good. I thought you were all blubber. Try it again."

Bones obeyed. This time he could feel the ache in his pitching muscle. He bit the inside of his cheek to keep from crying "Ow!"

The rest hour bell clanged. "No noise today," Chester warned them, "or you'll stay away from the play tonight."

"Chester, you got a big part?" Squid asked.

"He's the lead," Neil stated.

"It should be a good play," Leafy said accommodatingly. "*Champion* is a great story."

"It could have been, but that Weiman!" Chester groaned.

"He's OK," said Flip.

"He did a good job of adapting the story into a play," Chester admitted, "but he's directing it, too!"

Flip persisted. "He's put on some pretty good shows. What's wrong with him?"

"What's wrong?" Chester shouted. "There's no realism! When I punch, it's a play punch. I'm not supposed to touch anyone! What kind of a prize fighter am I gonna look like?" He extended his palms in an exasperated gesture. "Hubert Updegraff will be watching tonight! What's he gonna think of *me?*"

"Who's Hubert Updegraff?" Dick inquired in a bored tone, while he tested the hinges on his cot with his screwdriver.

"For your information . . ." Chester began. "No toys," he said, yanking the screwdriver out of Dick's hand.

"Gimme that." Dick reached for it.

"After rest hour." Chester stuck the tool in his pocket.

"All right. So who is this Updegraff character?" Now Dick sounded belligerent.

Chester looked smug. "My friend Hubert," he said,

"owns a hundred or more repertory theaters all over the country. And he's interested in me," the J.C. stated, thumbing his chest. "Get it?"

Bones leaned his head back against his pillow. Chester's worries were nothing compared to his own. Unless he got sick, he had to ask a girl to be his date on Field Day, two weeks away. But Field Day was the day of the tennis match, and getting sick would look as if he were chickening out against Neil. Playing the game was the least of his fears. He was even getting used to Chester's jibes. The worst he could do would be to get shellacked, Bones knew, but the thought of looking like a winded blimp with all those girls watching took more courage than he could muster.

12. The Champion

As Bones had expected, Chester stole the limelight that night. What he hadn't been prepared for, though, was the quality of the junior counselor's acting. The rest of the participating faculty, largely composed of high school English teachers who had had some practice in directing plays but little, if any, performing experience, appeared to be novices in contrast to Chesty. His timing, gestures, and verbal expression seemed professional.

There was one other exception. Miss Granby played her part well. She was the Champion's mother, and if Bones had not seen her name on the program, he would never have recognized her. The pigtailed brunette drama teacher had been transformed into a white-haired old lady. When Chester slugged her in the first act, she fell back as if truly hurt. Although the J.C.'s play punches looked real, the Champion's other victims, because of their poor acting, caused the audience no anxiety.

Bones was not surprised to see Chester surrounded by admirers after the final curtain. And neither was he surprised that girls dominated the cluster about him.

The boys from his cabin wanted to congratulate the J.C., too, but they hung back, waiting for the females to leave. Finally, the girls backed away in deference to Uncle Willie and a man who had been walking with the director.

"Must be Chester's father," Whitey stated.

Neil shook his head. "That's Updegraff."

Just then, the man waved his arms above his head in a cheering gesture. "Great! Great! What did I tell you, Frenzl!" The man reached for Chester's right arm and raised it into the air. "The champion! The real champion!"

For some reason, the J.C. seemed embarrassed by this ovation and moved a few steps away from Mr. Updegraff. This was not like Chester.

Bones found himself staring at the man in the gray pin-striped suit. His eyelids were lashless, and his eyes appeared glassy and lifeless, like those of a fish on ice in a supermarket. He reminded Bones of a smiling mackerel, this Updegraff character, the way he complimented Chester and then spouted streams of praise at Willard Frenzl. "Quite a setup you've got here. Must be worth a pretty penny."

Uncle Willie laughed. "A few pretty pennies."

"Oh?" Updegraff looked interested. "How much do you suppose the place is worth?"

That Updegraff looks familiar, Bones kept thinking, as he watched Uncle Willie rub his hand across his face. He looked tired, but he was trying to be a courteous host.

"Mr. Updegraff," the camp director finally said, "I have no idea how much this place is worth in dollars and cents. But I know it represents years of investment in loyal teaching. Some of our staff members were here twenty years ago, when Crescendo opened." He paused. "You're aware of our reputation?"

Mr. Updegraff nodded his head in answer to the director's question.

"I know!" Bones shouted.

"Know what?" his bunkmates asked.

Bones remained silent. Now he was almost positive this was the man he had seen with Chester by the Huber Building when he had been practicing his trombone in the woods. Unless he was mistaken, it was Mr. Updegraff who had said gruffly, "It better work!"

"What d'ye know?" the boys repeated.

"I know who I'm gonna ask for Field Day," Bones improvised.

Uncle Willie smiled in his direction. Then to Chester and Mr. Updegraff, he said, "They all make the plunge. It's good for these boys to have to choose a date. They don't hate girls as much as they like to think they do."

The other two smiled at Bones and chuckled appreciatively. Updegraff's grin gave Bones the creeps.

The boys from his cabin looked grim. Finally Dick spoke. "You getting soft in the head? Last year we hid on Field Day. We could do the same thing again."

"What about the tennis match?" Bones reminded him. Then to Neil, he added, "If the other guys hide, will you?"

"I hadn't thought about hiding," Neil answered, "but I hadn't thought about asking a date either."

Hank motioned to them. "Bedtime, cherubs."

As the boys ambled toward the bus, Whitey confessed to Bones, "I didn't want to say anything in front of the others, but I've already asked someone for Field Day."

Bones gasped. "We never discussed this. How did you get the nerve?"

"Oh, it was easy," said Whitey, grinning. "It's a girl in the flute section. She sits next to me in orchestra practice. All I did was say, 'About Field Day,' and she jumped right out of her seat and said, 'I'll go with you.' "

"That must be what they mean when they say women make men propose," Bones declared thoughtfully.

"Funny thing is," Whitey continued, "I hadn't meant to ask her—I was just sort of sounding her out."

"I'm glad you're stuck with a date, 'cause I want to go to Field Day, too. Not that I'm gonna beat Neil, but I want to see if I can make it tough for him to beat me. All that backboard practice ought to have some use."

Whitey agreed. Then he said, "Who'd you have in mind to ask?"

Bones threw up his hands. "I dunno."

"But, before, you said . . ."

"That was just a cover-up. What I really meant was that now I know where I saw that guy before, that Updegraff."

"He's supposed to be famous, according to Neil. You probably saw his picture in the newspaper."

Bones shook his head and proceeded to tell Whitey about witnessing Chester and Mr. Updegraff in a huddle near the drama cottage. "I don't like him," Bones concluded. "What's he doing here, anyway?"

"You don't even know him," Whitey protested.

"I just don't like him," Bones repeated. "He reminds me of a fish, a mackerel."

"A mackerel is good eating," said Whitey, laughing.

Bones wrinkled his nose. "If you like fish."

13. Rudderless

At the sound of reveille the next morning, feathers flew as the boys hurled their pillows at Chester. Then they leaped from their cots.

"Nice work, slugger!" Dick shouted.

"Good show, old man! Ouch!" Leafy hopped around, tugging at a splinter in his foot.

The other fellows yanked the J.C. out of bed. Hanging on to his arms and legs, they swung him, then heaved him back onto the cot. Squid pinned down his wrists. Dick sat on his legs. Neil stood back now and viewed the tomfoolery.

"Give up, killer?" Bones was preparing to tickle Chesty's ribs.

"I give up, guys. You're the champs."
The boys relaxed their hold.

Chester shook off his antagonists and jumped to the floor. "Wanna fight?" The junior counselor doubled his fists. Playfully, he jabbed at the boys.

"We didn't get a chance to congratulate you last night, but you sure made the show! You looked like a pro!" Hank voiced the sentiments of the cabin.

Chester was smiling as he glanced about, and Bones realized that for the first time the J.C. was aware of honest admiration on the faces of his cabin mates, for he said, "The play must have been a success 'cause it takes a lot to impress a bunch of roughnecks like you!"

"Mr. Updegraff must have enjoyed the performance, too," Leafy commented.

"He gave that impression." Neil was staring at his cousin with pride.

Chester's face clouded momentarily. Then he wheeled around and aimed the flat of his hand at Bones. "The next task at hand is to mold you into a perfect Bottom!"

Bones tried to shield his rump from the J.C.'s palm, but the counselor was too fast.

"By gosh!" exclaimed Chester. "That *Bottom* is diminishing!"

Hank winked at Bones. Then he said, "OK, boys, breakfast in ten minutes."

During lunch, Whitey let it seep out that he had asked a date for Field Day.

His announcement was met with cries of "Traitor!"

Bones came to his friend's rescue. "Neil and I are in the tennis match. We can't avoid Field Day, so we've got to get dates, too."

Dick looked glum. "But we don't."

"Squid is sure to win the track meet," Hank declared. "For the glory of the cabin, you guys have to attend Field Day."

"Oh, we can attend part of the time," Dick explained. "We'll just hide when they're counting partners. That's what we did last year."

"Nothing doing," the counselor insisted. "Either you get a date or you stay home."

Flip protested, "That means missing the wiener roast and . . ."

"The best meal at camp," interrupted Dick.

"There are plenty of girls in the orchestra," Whitey offered. "I can fix you guys up with a cellist, a couple of flutists, three harpists, or a bassoon player."

"I know. We'll draw for them," suggested Bones.

Hank turned to Bones. "Aren't you going to invite Pruneface?"

"Uh-uh. She's too stuck-up, and she's always yakking."

"OK," said Hank, "but what makes you think a flutist will be any better?"

"Your lips get tired from playing the flute," Whitey explained.

Hank pulled a pencil out of his hip pocket. He reached for a napkin. "We might as well get this over with." He nodded to Whitey. "You name them."

"Well, there's one big one, about Dick's height, and she plays off key . . ."

"OK," said Hank. "Number one, off key flutist. What's her name?"

"I don't know," Whitey confessed.

Hank chewed his pencil. "Do you know the other flutists' names?"

Whitey shook his head sheepishly.

"Well, what do they look like?" asked Dick. "We might as well hear the worst."

"One's got buckteeth. But she's wearing braces," Whitey hastened to reassure them. "By next year she'll be normal."

"Next year," Dick groaned. "Count me out. I'm better off with the concert master. She was born with braces!"

Chester, who had been too busy eating to enter the conversation before, suddenly snapped his fingers. "You guys leave this to Uncle Chesty. I can pick 'em," he announced, making a curved torso in the air with his hands. "And we've got some very cute girls in drama classes."

"Cute girls," scoffed Dick.

"All I want is a date that's so quiet I don't even know she's there," announced Bones.

Chester grabbed Hank's pencil and the napkin. "Bones —silent partner. Next request."

"Oh, I guess you can give me one that isn't too shrimpy," Squid said with a sigh of resignation.

Reluctantly, all save Whitey, who already had a date, made their desires known.

That afternoon Bones had more difficulty than usual concentrating in trombone class. He kept wondering what sort of a girl Chester would choose for him. If the J.C. still harbored a grudge over the turpentine episode, Bones could expect a horror. He knew he should have asked his own date, but he didn't relish the idea.

During the last period of the day, free swim, Bones and Whitey obtained permission to take a sail and try their luck at fishing.

Paul, the head waterfront counselor, told them to be back in forty-five minutes. When he handed them a rusty coffee can filled with limp minnows floating in stagnant water, he said, "If you wiggle your rod, maybe the fish will think they're alive."

As they shoved the boat off the sandy lake shore, Bones remarked, "Chester will probably fix me up with a two-headed witch who talks like a parrot."

"I'll lend you my earplugs," Whitey offered magnanimously.

Bones hoisted the mainsail of the small sloop, and Whitey went forward to fix the jib. They let the sails and rudder swing free so that the boat pointed south into the wind.

"Let's head straight out," Whitey suggested. "Then we'll be at a right angle with the wind." The sails caught a breeze from the east.

With his eyes averted, Bones felt for a minnow. "I really don't like to fish," he confessed, making a face as he took his hand out of the can and wiped the slime off on his T-shirt.

"You handle the tiller, then." Whitey reached for the rod.

"Careful!" Whitey shrieked.

Bones could feel the wind change direction. He ducked in time to escape the boom when it crashed around to the other side.

"Point north," Whitey ordered.

Bones yanked the tiller to his right. He heard the crackle of wood splitting. "Whitey!" he screamed. The gudgeons that held the rudder in place had broken off and sunk. Bones was left powerless to steer, holding the tiller in midair while the rudder trailed in the water behind them. He hauled the rudder into the boat. "Now what?"

"Drop the sails and try the paddle. There's no way of attaching the rudder without the metal fittings."

Bones tossed the rudder and tiller into the cockpit. "Where's the paddle?"

"It should be there somewhere."

Bones crawled into the forward end of the boat. "There isn't any paddle."

"There's got to be a paddle," Whitey insisted. "That's one of the safety regulations."

"What should we do?" Bones asked, as they drifted farther and farther away from the shore. They were beyond yelling distance now. The second float was a white speck behind them.

"We could swim," Whitey suggested.

"You mean desert the ship like rats?" Bones feigned indignation.

The sun had begun its evening descent, and even earlier, when he reached for the rudder, the lake had felt mighty cold. Also he was not sure of the distance they would have to swim. The breeze died, and a loon screeched into the stillness.

"I'm hungry," declared Bones, kicking the can of minnows.

"I think I've got a small bite," Whitey said suddenly. "You like raw sunfish?"

Bones uttered a choking noise. "You *know* I don't like fish, not even *cooked* fish dunked in *chocolate* syrup!"

"I'll have to try that," said Whitey, "next time we have boiled codfish. That Wirtz glop is strong chocolate!"

"Shut up!" Bones growled. "I might die out here without having tasted that gooey stuff!"

"They'll be looking for us." Whitey sounded unalarmed. "You think this camp will risk its reputation, and let us drown? What would the parents say? Who would send their kids to a camp that left two kids stranded in the middle of Rainbow Lake?"

"All I can say," Bones declared, "is that this is a big lake, and my stomach tells me it's suppertime. Why, they might not find us till tomorrow after breakfast!"

Whitey was silent now. His rod was bending.

"You've got something!" Bones shouted. That fish must have been hungry, even hungrier than he was, to go for a dead minnow.

Whitey tightened his line, then stood up and leaned over the side.

"You're tipping the boat," Bones protested.

Whitey continued to reel in the line, paying no heed to Bones, who moved to the opposite side to act as ballast.

"A pike!" Whitey shouted, as the sharp-toothed, yellowish fish fought in midair.

With mock solemnity, Bones declared, "And to think no one will ever know."

The boys were still. A faint *put-put* was coming from shore. Or was it just the ripple of the lake slapping against the hull?

14. A Meeting with the Boss

The *put-put* became louder when the boys saw a small motor launch heading toward them. As the boat drew near, Paul and Hank were discernible.

"You scoundrels!" Paul yelled. "I told you to be back in forty-five minutes. Uncle Willie is coughing steam!"

"We're stuck!" Whitey called back.

Paul steered the launch alongside the sloop.

"We didn't do it on purpose. The rudder broke off," Bones explained.

"Why didn't you use the paddle?" Paul asked, tossing them a tow line.

"We couldn't find a paddle," Bones replied.

Paul's eyes opened wide. He gaped at Hank. "What'll

I say? The boss is gonna have my neck! There's supposed to be a paddle in every sailboat."

"One of the kids must have been fooling around with it," Hank suggested.

"I suppose so." Paul dug his fingers into his scalp. "But, I'm responsible . . ."

"You can't control every kid's prank," Hank interceded, trying to soothe the waterfront counselor.

When the launch reached the dock, Whitey raised the centerboard. Then the two boys jumped into the water and shoved the sailboat onto the sand.

"Oh boy, am I hungry!"

"You'll have to stay that way a little longer," Paul told Bones. "The three of us have a date with the chief."

"I feel . . . well, maybe it's like going before the *Wizard of Oz*," Bones announced with awe.

There was an oriental carpet in the waiting room of Uncle Willie's office. A gray-haired secretary with a stingy smile dropped the phone when she saw them. Without a word, she knocked on the director's door.

"Come in," he said.

The secretary motioned for them to enter.

"Thank God." Willard Frenzl sat slumped in a black leather chair behind his desk. His tan freckles looked out of place on his pallid complexion, but after a brief glance at the boys, the color returned to his face, and the frown on his forehead disappeared. "You're all right, I take it?"

They nodded. The boys found themselves staring into Uncle Willie's weary green eyes. He had an honest face, and when the corners of his lips turned up, Whitey and Bones relaxed.

The director turned to Paul. "Have these boys eaten?"

Bones broke out into a grin as the counselor replied, "No, sir."

"Well, then you hustle them up some refreshments, something extra special." Turning to the boys, he continued, "Start from the beginning. How did all this happen?"

The boys related their adventure, constantly interrupting each other. When the tale was told, Uncle Willie commended them, "You boys were very wise. As long as you stayed with the boat, you were in no danger, for, as Paul explained to me, the hull was fiberglass and wouldn't sink. Did you know this?"

The boys shook their heads. Then Bones said, "But wooden boats float, too, even when they turn over."

"Usually," the director conceded. He frowned and continued. "I don't understand why that rudder broke off. All our boats are overhauled every spring. We've never had anything like this happen before."

For Paul's sake, the boys did not mention the missing paddle, and Uncle Willie did not press them further.

When the two counselors returned with loaded trays, both containing apple pie à la mode, Bones said blissfully, "This makes everything worthwhile."

Uncle Willie seemed to enjoy watching them eat. After they had finished, he said to Paul, "I'd like a word alone with you."

Bones said, "Whatever happened, sir, it wasn't his fault."

"I know that," the director replied kindly. "We just have to straighten out one or two things."

Outside, Hank explained, "Uncle Willie sent the waterfront staff and a few other counselors in search of you kids. He was afraid of a panic if the other campers found out you were missing, so everything went on as usual." The counselor grinned, before adding, "And you're just in time for the second half of the dance recital."

"Too bad you found us so soon." Bones found it easy to

joke now that he was back. Then he remembered his fishing rod and asked if he could get it.

Hank shook his head. "In the morning."

"Someone might take it," Bones persisted.

"Oh, all right." Hank gave them his flashlight. "I'll wait here."

"Anything to get out of that dance recital!" Whitey declared as they walked to the beach.

"The heck with the rod, you jerk. It's the fish I want!" Bones's eyes danced. "I thought it would make Chester's bed feel real cozy."

"Do you think we should do it now," Whitey asked, "when the guy is getting almost human?"

"He likes the attention," Bones reassured his friend. "He'll feel neglected if we don't do something pretty soon."

Whitey didn't look convinced. "He's gonna know it's you."

"He won't be sure, unless you tell him."

"What are you going to carry the fish back in, and how are you going to sneak it into Chester's bed?"

"I'll show you," Bones said confidently.

Bones lifted the pike by its tail and held it at arm's length. "You wanna slip it in your T-shirt?" he asked hopefully.

"Not me!" Whitey responded.

"I thought you liked fish."

"To eat." Whitey emphasized the last word.

"Then I guess I'll have to wear it." Bones screwed up his mouth to close his nostrils. He stretched his neck and looked at the sky as he slid the pike down inside his shirt. "Ugh! It's slimy." The fish was moist and slippery against his bare chest. It skidded around and rested crosswise above his belt.

Bones folded his arms across his midriff. "How does it look?"

After Whitey assured him that it didn't show, the boys started to walk back.

"The rod!" Whitey reminded Bones. "I'll run back and get it. You're in no shape to run."

"What took you so long?" Hank inquired when the boys returned.

Silently, Whitey and Bones shrugged their shoulders. Then scowling, they trailed Hank to the outdoor bowl. An usher handed them a program as they entered. The counselor made them walk more than halfway down the slanted path until they saw their group. All the while, Bones covered the outline of the fish with his folded arms to keep it from sliding around to his back.

As they sat down, Hank leaned toward Bones. "There's your girl friend."

Sure enough, there was Pruneface, her black bangs and black straight hair flying as she and two other girls danced to some offbeat modern music.

"There's no melody," Bones announced. "They could just as easily dance to numbers." The thought made him chuckle, and the pike began to flap against his stomach.

Whitey shoved his elbow against Bones's arm. "You're beginning to stink."

"I thought even your best friends didn't tell you that." Whitey was right, though. The fishy odor was becoming noticeable. The heat from his body was probably encouraging it, Bones thought. He felt sweaty and sticky, and he ached for the performance to be over.

While the audience applauded the finale, Bones jested to Whitey, "Do you suppose Pruneface would like a bouquet?" That was one way of disposing of the fish.

Hank hustled his gang toward the bus, but Bones kept lagging behind for fear they would smell his secret.

Hank became impatient. "Come on there, Cluett. Shake the fat." To oblige, Bones trotted with his arms still folded over his middle.

"You run as if you've eaten a load of green apples. What's the matter?" the counselor asked. "You got a stomach ache or something?"

"Just a little something." Bones could not resist making the last remark.

Hank looked worried. "Ever have your appendix removed?"

Bones shook his head. "But it's nothing like that," he assured him. This was no time for a checkup with the camp doctor.

Bones's biggest problem arose when all the kids began undressing. If only Hank would leave the cabin, the way Chester usually did, to gab with the other counselors.

"Cluett, get moving." Hank was at his heels.

Bones grabbed his pajamas from under his pillow and went into the bathroom.

"You modest all of a sudden?" Squid asked when Bones bolted the door.

He needed some ice. This fish *was* beginning to smell!

For the first time in his life, Bones applied a wash cloth to his body without being told. He changed into his pajamas, threw the fish on the floor of the shower, and drew the curtain. He would retrieve the pike later when the coast was clear for him to plant it. He almost pitied Chester. This fish would not improve with age!

His hiding place had come in handy for another prank, Bones remembered, and then it occurred to him that Hank might take a shower tonight!

15. A Matter of a Few Inches

Shortly after taps, Hank left the cabin. Bones returned to the bathroom. The fishy stench nauseated him. Before he removed the pike from the shower, he sprayed the room and the fish with pine-scented air freshener. But still his stomach turned as he reached for the pike. He held it stiffly by the tail and tiptoed back across the creaky cabin floor.

"Phew! That smell! Whatcha doing?" asked Squid.

Bones did not answer. He tucked the fish between Chester's sheets, then ran into the bathroom to wash his hands.

Every time the counselor on patrol flashed his light through the screen door, Bones became rigid. His J.C.

must be out on a date tonight, Bones decided, after the third false alarm. Finally, Bones could feel the excitement of the day ebb away. His eyelids collapsed and he dozed off, reassuring himself that he smelled fish only because he knew it was in Chester's bed.

Good old Flip was blowing reveille next morning. Squid, with his face buried in his pillow and one arm outstretched, pleaded, "Give me five more minutes. I haven't finished my dream."

Maybe Chester likes dead fish, Bones thought, as the junior counselor bounced out of bed generating sunshine and happy chatter. Bones had never seen him in such a good mood.

While Whitey crawled under the lower bunk to look for his sneaker, Bones whispered, "See, he's flattered by all the attention."

"Something fishy goin' on," murmured Whitey. "You wait."

Bones did not have long to wait. In drama class, Miss Granby announced, "Our first dress rehearsal."

Chester, it seemed, was in charge of wardrobing the boys. When he came toward Bones with a roll of balding black velvet under one arm and beckoned to him with a pair of long purple stockings, the J.C.'s eyes were sparkling, though his lips tried hard not to grin.

Bones prophesied that Chester would get even with him in his own subtle way. Rather than make a fool of himself by acknowledging another practical joke, the J.C. would see that *Bottom* appeared even more ridiculous than Shakespeare had intended. Chester would gloat while the rest of the camp guffawed at Bones's expense.

Bones took off the camp uniform. He held up black velvet bloomers trimmed with stripes of gold braiding. When he put them on, he discovered to his dismay that they barely reached the beginning of his thighs.

"I'm naked!" he screamed. He tried to stretch the elastic that pinched his legs and caused a roll of fat to appear below them, but the puffy-styled bloomers just made it around his hips, and there was no material left to pull.

"Better than I thought," Chester declared. "At least you're in them. Good thing these pants flare," he added.

"Not very flattering," Bones complained. He didn't need ballooning bloomers. "They won't close!" he announced triumphantly. They would have to find something else—maybe a pair of trousers. He would even settle for knickers, like Whitey.

"We can fix that," Chester assured him, as he attempted to join the bloomers. "We'll string a few safety pins together. It's just a matter of a few inches."

"A few inches!" Bones protested. "The whole thing's too small. It'll stop my circulation!"

"We can stretch the elastic," Chester continued calmly. "Even break it. Now try the tunic."

The tunic must have seen more wear than the pants, for large patches of it were threadbare. There was no decoration save a huge red satin ribbon attached to the collar and undoubtedly meant to be tied Lord Fauntleroy fashion. Bones shuddered. A big red bow beneath his chins would complete the caricature.

"Put the tunic on," Chester said impatiently. Bones realized his J.C. could hardly wait to see him in full attire.

Bones picked at the lint before trying to put his arm into the sleeve. "They must have put this in the washing machine."

Chester glared at him. "Hurry up. I'm not your personal valet. I've got other kids to dress."

It was easy to stick his hand in the jacket because the

upper part of the sleeves puffed, but as he worked his fingers down, he heard the seams split. By pulling and tugging, Chester manipulated the sleeve while Bones did nothing but sweat.

With resignation, Bones held out his other arm. "You've encased one sausage."

When the buttons did not meet the buttonholes, Chester said, "We'll have to move the buttons." However, when the purple stockings only reached the top of his knees, even Chester was stumped.

Bones jested, "You can always wrap me in bandages."

"That's it!"

Bones could hear the J.C. running down the stage steps while he stood there imprisoned in black velvet, soaked with perspiration, and without a notion of how to escape wearing this costume. Chester returned with a bolt of white gauze and pins. "I just want to measure this. We can dye the cloth and staple it to the stockings."

"It'll never match," Bones suggested hopefully.

"It'll do," Chester mumbled with a pin in his mouth.

In desperation Bones asked, "How would you like to look like this?"

"Oh," Chester said, looking him in the eye for a second, "I wouldn't." Then he snickered and exclaimed, "But I couldn't look like this!"

16. Midsummer Nightmare

At about noon on the day of the play, the Cluett family arrived at camp to witness Bones's dramatic debut. This was a bonus he had not expected. He decided not to refer to Carolyn's gift. If he were tactful, she might persuade Chester to let him wear long pants!

Midge had embarrassed Bones right away by kissing him in front of the camp bus. That was bad enough, but even Carolyn was ready to slug her when she raised her voice and asked, "Where's Chester?"

Hank introduced himself to the Cluetts, and Mr. Cluett took the opportunity to praise him. "My son wrote that he had a great counselor, and I must admit," he said, pulling at his chin and appraising Bones, "the results look great.

One thing puzzles me, however," Mr. Cluett added with a serious face, "how did you get Bones to lose weight, and still keep his affection?"

Hank laughed.

Bones could tell that his father and his counselor had clicked. He wondered what his dad would think of his junior counselor. Bones decided to capitalize on Carolyn's presence to ingratiate himself with the J.C. He would have to work fast. He saw Chester a few yards up the road, leaning against the door of a black sports car. He excused himself from his family.

When he approached the car, Bones was not surprised to see Hubert Updegraff in the driver's seat. He heard the last few words of Chester's conversation, ". . . easier said than done. I've got to be careful."

Careful about what, Bones wondered, as Updegraff announced guardedly, "A friend of yours."

Chester looked up at him in a startled sort of way. "Anything wrong?"

Bones shook his head. "I just wanted you to meet my family."

"Oh." Chester's eyes lit up. "They're here for the play."

"See you later," Updegraff said, starting the motor of his car.

As they walked together, Bones said, "You've got to find different pants for me. My family will be chagrined if I walk on the stage looking like Little Lord Fauntleroy."

"Don't worry," Chester hurried to assure him. "You won't look like Lord Fauntleroy. You'll make a perfect Bottom. Even Shakespeare would appro—"

"There's Chester!" Midge interrupted, running up to them.

Chester stared at Midge in amazement. "How do you know my name?"

A look of disappointment flashed across her face. More kindly this time, Chester asked, "And who are you?"

"Bones's sister, of course," Midge stated flatly. "You look just like your picture."

The junior counselor appeared to be in a state of shock. He stood still, his mouth agape as his eyes traveled from Midge to Bones. When he regained his composure, he turned to the grinning Bones and exclaimed, "Some joke!"

Bones wore an innocent expression now. He was almost tempted not to introduce the J.C. to the rest of his family, but Midge ran back to the Cluetts and announced Chester's arrival.

As Bones made the introductions, both Chester's relief and Carolyn's feelings of awkwardness were evident. Bones really felt sorry for Midge—when Carolyn got her alone, yipe!

After Whitey greeted the Cluetts, Hank said, "It's time to go, boys."

"Let my father drive us back," Bones pleaded.

The boys were permitted to ride in the family car. Mr. Cluett drove carefully behind the yellow bus, trying to avoid the deeper ruts on the winding dirt road.

"How's the food?" Mrs. Cluett inquired in a tone that required a negative reply.

"Just awful."

Bones thought his mother looked pleased as she said, "I'm planning your homecoming meal. Steak, French fries, those little peas that you—"

Bones groaned.

"Stop teasing the boy," his father commanded. "They put him on a diet, and they're doing a good job."

"But he's growing and he needs—"

"I'm not worried about his body," Mr. Cluett said

gruffly. "That's been well-nourished. How's the trombone coming? Can you play 'The Star Spangled Banner'?" Mr. Cluett's tone called for an enthusiastic response.

"I've almost perfected the scale," Bones declared, realizing his father would not appreciate his small triumph. "And I'm only in the woods for half the period now," Bones added cheerily.

"In the woods?" Mr. Cluett appeared perplexed for a minute. "Oh, you mean in the dark. Well, I guess it will take time to shape you into a virtuoso."

"It'll take more than time." His dad had better not expect too much. "The woods aren't dark," Bones went on to explain. "We only have classes in the daytime."

His parents laughed.

" 'In the woods' and 'in the dark' are expressions that mean you don't exactly know what's going on," his father informed him.

"Oh." Bones rolled his eyes. In that case he was really in the woods all the time, he thought, but he said, "You see, I practice outside for the first half of the period, and then Pierce lets me come in so he can hear what I've been practicing."

"And you used to be out there all the time. I get it," replied Mr. Cluett.

"Well, I don't like it," objected Mrs. Cluett. "You poor boy. Out there all alone."

"Oh, Mother." Carolyn's voice registered disgust.

When they arrived at the boys' camp, Bones pulled Carolyn aside. "Help me," he begged.

"It sounds like a matter of life or death."

"Almost," Bones acknowledged. "Chester likes you. I can tell by the way he was looking at you when he didn't think you were watching."

"Maybe." Her face flushed as she said, "The way Midge

behaved, I don't see how he could like me or any other member of this family."

"Oh, he likes you," Bones repeated. "I bet he'd do anything you asked."

"Like what?" Carolyn sounded suspicious. She was quick at sizing up situations.

"You don't want me to embarrass you tonight?" Bones said.

"I've been embarrassed enough for one day already, thank you."

"Then you've got to help me."

"Why did you fix me up with this joker anyway? So that you'd have an in with him?"

"You were the one who asked me to!" Bones declared indignantly. "You told me to hang your picture on my wall."

"Well, that isn't the way Chester—"

Bones interrupted, "I was clever. I made him want to write to you."

"Um-hm." Carolyn did not look convinced. "Go on."

"Do you want me to wear bloomers that come up to here?" Bones pointed to the top of his thigh. "There'll be hundreds of people in the audience!"

"What does that have to do with Chester?"

"Chester is a drama counselor, and he's in charge of *my* costume!"

"So that's it. Make friends with Chester, and save face for Bones Cluett!"

"Not my face. Spare my legs!" Bones wailed. "Suggest that I wear trousers, knickers, anything. Say Dad will be furious and probably complain to the camp. Tell Chester my wearing bloomers will get him into trouble."

Carolyn laughed. "You mean threaten him. But I don't even know him," she protested.

"You do, too," Bones insisted.

"Not really." To mollify Bones, she said, "I'll see what I can do."

Bones decided to cement relations between his J.C. and Carolyn. He went up to Chester, who was sitting on the cabin steps. "My sister thinks you're swell," he said, putting syrup into his voice.

"Which one?" asked Chester, patting the top of Bones's head, but soon after, he noticed the J.C. walking toward Carolyn.

Bones was grinning as he pulled open the cabin door. "Any chance of my family eating lunch with us?" he inquired of Hank.

"If it's not too late to make arrangements," the counselor replied. "Why don't you run over to the mess hall and ask."

Bones arranged to have his family lunch in the boys' dining quarters. His friends were quieter than usual and only spoke when questions were directed at them.

During the meal, Carolyn's face was solemn. She was either worrying about her mission or wondering what Midge would do to annoy her further. Probably the latter, Bones decided, for every now and then Carolyn would cast dirty looks at her sister. Bones guessed it was because Midge chewed with her mouth open and didn't wait to swallow her mashed potatoes before chattering.

His younger sister was the only one who seemed at ease, and as a result she monopolized the conversation. "Is that all you eat?" she asked, when Bones had finished his scanty meal.

Carolyn could not contain herself any longer. "You're dribbling gravy, you little monster. Now leave Bones alone."

Unabashed by her reprimand, Midge turned to Hank.

"Why didn't *you* write to Carolyn?" She smiled sweetly and asked, "Did Bones tell you she was a grouch?"

Hank returned Midge's smile and replied, "Bones only says nice things about his sisters."

Midge lifted her chin importantly, and then Bones thought she pressed her luck, for she inquired, "What did he say about me?"

With diplomacy, Hank answered, "He said that you were very smart and that you were as pretty as a movie star."

For the rest of the meal, Midge appeared to be thinking about what Hank had said and, Bones suspected, trying to act the part.

When they rose to return their trays, Bones observed Chester gallantly reach for Carolyn's. He took his mother's tray, and Hank tried to take Midge's, but she insisted upon carrying it herself.

Bones had to say good-by to his family after lunch. He arranged to meet them at his guitar class.

Chester was not in the cabin during rest period. Bones hoped Carolyn was working on him.

As things turned out, the reverse had occurred. Chester convinced Carolyn that Bones would be a sensation as Bottom and that his costume must not be altered.

"You'll be sorry," Bones warned her when she told him this.

"Good luck," Carolyn said with a smile. "I'm anxious to see this play."

Bones put his hand to his forehead. "I think I have a fever."

"Oh, no you don't, Bones Cluett! We drove up especially to see you in *A Midsummer Night's Dream.*"

"It's my midsummer nightmare!" Bones groaned. He knew Chester was getting even with him for sticking the fish in his bed, but he couldn't tell Carolyn that.

The day passed too swiftly. The night came too fast. Bones found himself in the wings of the Huber Theater, surrounded by actors.

"You're on," Miss Granby announced, waving the script at him.

Bones's legs wouldn't move. Chester pushed him forward, and he stumbled onto the stage.

The audience howled when Bones entered. He had no choice. He straightened up in time to respond to his cue, and then he overplayed his part, burlesquing for all he was worth. He buried his face when he said, "And I may hide my face . . ." and squeaked ". . . I'll speak in a monstrous little voice, 'Thisne, Thisne!' "

The footlights were an asset, blinding Bones and preventing him from seeing the faces in the audience. He acted as if he were in a trance, oblivious to everything but his cues and his part. To his surprise, his voice came out loud and clear, and his replies were so well timed that he felt as if a ventriloquist were doing the acting. His gestures, too, and his overacting seemed to be someone else's motions.

When the first act was over and he had *not* goofed, Bones began to relax. Chester and Miss Granby assured the cast that everything was going well.

In the third act, Bones wore a papier-mâché donkey's head, which, under the powerful stage lighting, caused him to sweat and made his grease paint run. His nose began to itch, and he felt a sneeze coming. He went through his lines squelching the sneeze.

"Louder," Miss Granby called from the wings. Bones pushed up the chin of the mask so that the mouth opening would coincide with his lips.

At this point in the play, Titania, Queen of the Fairies, had been drugged with love juice so that she would be-

come enamored with the first being she encountered, and the first being she saw was Bottom, grotesque in his donkey's mask, purple stockings, and skimpy bloomers. Now Titania was speaking to him. "What angel wakes me from my flowery bed?"

The mask bobbed as Bones blasted a mighty "Kerchoo!"

The audience roared. Fortunately, his own mirth was hidden by the donkey's head, but he could not stop laughing, and he had to speak.

"Take a deep breath," Miss Granby advised from the wings.

It worked. Bones was able to continue until Titania said:

> *"Mine ear is much enamour'd of thy note;*
> *So is mine eye enthralled to thy shape . . ."*

The mask began to rock again. This time Bones took hold of himself, opening his mouth as wide as his jail permitted. During the balance of the play Bones stretched his mouth open and pinched his arm till it burned in order to be able to answer without a giggle each time Titania made love to him.

A ballet—girls in tulle flitting about to Mendelssohn's music played by the camp orchestra—ended the performance. Watching the finale, Bones was filled with such a sense of relief that he almost appreciated the classical composition.

"Wonderful!" the drama teacher shouted when the curtain lowered.

The audience applauded for at least ten minutes. The cast took four curtain calls. Bones was happy when the clapping ceased. He unbuttoned his tunic and tugged at his sleeves, but Miss Granby and Chester were needed to excavate him from his costume, and both actor and apparel suffered in the process.

Mr. Updegraff came backstage looking for Chester. When he saw Bones, he said, "I enjoyed your performance. Quite a get-up," he added. Bones acknowledged the praise with a grin.

Bones was tying his shoe when his father appeared. "May I bring the ladies backstage?" Mr. Cluett asked Chester.

"Sure," the J.C. replied. "The fellows are all dressed now." He smiled and nodded toward Bones. "It took a while to dig him out."

Mr. Cluett went to the stage entrance to call his family.

"It was marvelous!" Carolyn gushed.

Chester seemed grateful for her enthusiasm.

"That was quite a garb you designed for my son," Mr. Cluett informed the J.C. "I think Bones stole the show!" he added proudly.

Carolyn glanced triumphantly at Bones while Mr. Updegraff said, "That's your boy? He's very talented."

Mrs. Cluett beamed at Mr. Updegraff, and Chester introduced the man to Bones's family.

"No wonder you looked so familiar," Mr. Cluett declared to Hubert Updegraff. "I saw your picture in the paper yesterday."

"Oh, that Florida deal." Mr. Updegraff bit his lip thoughtfully.

"You got a good buy," Mr. Cluett continued.

"Well, that resort was on the brink of bankruptcy," Hubert Updegraff explained, gesturing with his hands. "They were lucky to salvage anything. The place was in a deplorable state."

"Even so," Mr. Cluett said, pursuing the conversation, "it's valuable property."

"I guess so," Updegraff conceded.

Mrs. Cluett entered the discussion. "Are you going to build any repertory theaters in Vermont? It would be wonderful to have one near the camp."

Bones watched Updegraff flash his phony smile at Mrs. Cluett. "Nothing in the near future, dear lady."

"Then you're just here for a visit," Bones's mother concluded.

"That's right," the man replied. "I came to see my protégé, Chester."

The J.C. received looks of admiration from Mr. and Mrs. Cluett and Carolyn, but Bones was wondering just what kind of a protégé Chester really was. Obviously, an important man like Hubert Updegraff had more to do than visit a talented youngster.

17. Field Day

This is ridiculous, Bones told himself, as the Cluett Chevy rolled away down the dirt road. He wasn't homesick before they came, yet watching them depart depressed him. Chester was standing next to him and must have sensed his doldrums, for he said, "You've got a nice family."

"Yeah. I even miss Midge, now that she's gone," Bones admitted.

There was an expression of longing on Chester's face as he declared, "It must be wonderful having sisters."

"Wonderful?" This thought had never occurred to Bones. "I'd rather they were brothers."

"You won't when you're older," the J.C. predicted.

Bones stared at Chester with curiosity. He didn't sound like the same guy who had baited him on the train. He sounded more like Hank. He's being nice 'cause he wants me to put in a good word for him with Carolyn, Bones reasoned.

"You think I'm kidding, don't you?" Chester continued.

"No," Bones replied. "It's just that no one ever said that to me before." He added, "All boys in your family, I take it."

"It's just me," Chesty explained, "and my mother."

"Oh." Bones waited for the J.C. to speak.

"My father died two years ago, and our house is kind of empty."

"That must be lonely for you," Bones said. He felt uncomfortable sympathizing with Chesty. The J.C. had always seemed so independent.

To lighten the conversation, Bones announced, "Your cousin is going to make hash out of a 'Meatball' tomorrow."

Chester responded with a chuckle. "That's not what Hank tells me."

"He doesn't expect me to win," Bones confessed. "But he sure has worked hard to make a tennis player out of me."

"That guy is all right," Chester acknowledged. "I thought Hank was a bit pompous when we first met. You know, a 'holier than thou' type, but he's sincere. He really means what he says."

It sounded as if the two counselors had become friends. Bones wondered if Hank had told Chester to ignore the fish incident. It was the sort of thing the older counselor might have done, but Bones did not feel like inquiring. Instead he asked, "How does Neil like camp?"

"He's coming alone fine," Chester answered. "Hank and I had a long talk about Neil."

Bones was thinking of his own conversation with Hank. He ventured, "You're Neil's hero."

"I know." Chesty looked down as if ashamed and ground his sneaker in the dirt. "I'm afraid I've taken advantage of him."

Chester's admission surprised Bones. Hank must have been responsible for this realization, too, Bones decided. It was funny how that guy made you do the right thing, just by being interested in you. When Dick Bowman had offered to open a can of Wirtz Syrup for Bones, he had refused it because somehow he couldn't let Hank down. It was the first time in his life that he had voluntarily denied himself anything with chocolate on the label.

"I think you're going to like your date," the J.C. informed Bones now with a sly smile.

"What's her name? What does she look like?" Bones asked eagerly.

"It's a surprise."

"I hate surprises!" exclaimed Bones.

Although he pestered Chester all evening, the J.C. imparted no further information.

That night Bones slept fitfully. He dreamed that he was dodging Neil's serves instead of returning them and that his date was a giant eleven feet tall with a cavernous mouth that never closed. It was a relief to awaken on the morning of Field Day.

After breakfast, the boys were tidying the cabin for inspection. As Bones scoured the sink, he glanced into the mirror. He wondered if he should comb his hair for the occasion. He noticed that the other boys were making surreptitious preparations.

When the cabin passed inspection, Hank scrutinized his charges. He peered into Dick Bowman's ear. "It's going to take steel wool to make you shine."

The counselor filled the sink with soapy water and watched each boy scrub himself. If their efforts were halfhearted, Hank grabbed the washrag and rubbed till they were chafed. Then he sent them to Chester, who smeared white liquid on their scalps and plastered their hair against their heads.

"Nobody will recognize us," Bones complained, glancing about the cabin at his well-groomed companions.

"That's the idea," Hank announced, opening the door and motioning to them.

With pride, the counselors watched the intermediate boys ascend the bus, while the boys themselves slyly glanced at one another in embarrassment.

Bones sat behind Bob Holburg, the driver. To cover his feelings of awkwardness, he asked, "Ever find out how the fire started?"

The counselor shook his head. "Uncle Willie and I discussed it. We chalked it up to carelessness." He scowled and continued, "Though I don't see how a cigarette butt could land in a bus."

Bones leaned back and thought about his encounter with the female fire brigade. He wondered which one of the water carriers would turn out to be his date. Then he realized that he probably wouldn't be able to identify her any more than she would be able to distinguish him. Living with Carolyn had taught him that curlers and war paint camouflaged more than soap and water could uncover.

Both sexes entered the concert bowl, the girls on the left side, the boys on the right.

From the podium, Uncle Willie's head bobbed and he smiled like an unbearded Santa Claus. "No speeches," he assured them. "This is a day of pure pleasure."

The seniors cheered. The younger boys looked ago-
nized.

When Chesty said, "C'mon, I'll introduce you to your
dates," Bones clutched his tennis racket with both hands
and gritted his teeth. The J.C. led the contingent while
Hank flanked the rear.

"Prison camp," Dick muttered.

As they marched toward the intermediate girls, the
boys stared straight ahead, affecting indifference to the
appraising female glances.

"Meatball! You're with me!"

Oh, no, Bones thought. He did not need eyes to verify
who his partner was. Pruneface's strident voice could
never be disguised, even if her hair was set in a wiggle of
curls. His eyes left Prue to seek confirmation from Chester.

Looking smug, the J.C. said, "I knew you would be
pleased." He moved on to pair off the others.

"The silent partner," Bones grumbled under his breath.
He forced a dazed smile and felt as if he had just swal-
lowed a frog.

To break the silence, Prue asked, "Would you rather I
called you Bottom?"

Bones wiped the perspiration off his forehead with his
shirtsleeve. "You must take drama," he said foolishly.

Pruneface took pity on him. "If it's any comfort," she
began, "I selected you from Chester's list."

Though he would not have admitted it, Bones felt flattered. Moreover, he knew Prue had enough poise for both
of them, and they would not be stuck for want of conversation. Unfortunately, as she chattered on, he realized that
the dream about the date with a mouth that never closed
had materialized. He became apprehensive. How much of
the rest of his dream would come true?

He sought out Neil for reassurance. Neil was walking rigidly behind a slight blond girl. He looked even less secure than Bones. He's hardly capable of power tennis today, Bones consoled himself, as they walked toward the red clay courts.

Chivalry was not dead at Camp Crescendo. The girls battled it out on the courts first, while the male contestants sweated and waited their turn.

The senior girls were practiced players, Bones observed. "I'm glad I don't have to play against her," he said, watching a tall competitor ace her opponent along the center line, using the American twist serve.

"Her father is a pro," Pruneface informed him. "She'll probably win 6-love. The game is just a formality."

"The other one is a good sport to play. She sure is taking a beating."

"Someone had to be the goat," Prue explained. "They don't hand out awards without some pretence of competition."

Bones sighed. Soon he would be the sacrificial offering for another champ. What a sight that would be! The husky Bones, for all his diet, the still well-rounded Bottom, would be bombarded by aces, befuddled by lobs, and ducking swift net volleys delivered by the shy, wiry Neil, who would undoubtedly be acclaimed hero of the day.

The camp audience watched Bones and Neil shake hands before the match.

"You call it," Neil requested.

"Smooth," Bones replied, hoping he would not have to serve first.

Neil held the racket head perpendicular to the court, then giving the handle a twist, he stepped back and announced, "Smooth it is."

Bones wondered if this was really true. He looked warily

at the senior who was acting as linesman to his right. Then
he stepped carefully behind the white line. He threw up
the ball. It veered to the right instead of going straight up
above his left shoulder. Bones let the ball drop. He
stooped to retrieve it and caught a wink from Hank
through the wire fence. Take your time, Bones said to
himself, as his teacher had often repeated.

Perhaps because he was not expected to win, Bones decided to make every stroke count.

Keep him on the defensive, Bones told himself, and his
forehand curved out to his far right, which was Neil's left,
his backhand. As long as he kept Neil from the net, he had
a chance.

Neil stepped back and waited for Bones's shot to go out,
only to see it land on the line when it was too late for him
to get into position.

A tingle of pleasure went through Bones as he realized
that he had fooled his opponent, but he did not allow
himself complacency or rely on one tactic. He aimed for
the corners, and as Neil ran for the opposite corner, sometimes he scored a point by sending the ball back to the
place from which it came.

Still, form and skill were his competitor's artillery.
Bones's arm buckled against Neil's potent forehand, and
he had trouble returning the boy's first serve. He either
fluffed it or sent back a creampuff shot that Neil killed
without effort. As the tournament proceeded, Bones lost
ground steadily. Although his tactics saved him from dis-
grace, he now understood that a tennis victory over an
adept player meant having both a power serve and a forehand smash that could be depended upon, not the erratic
stabs at glory he was able to perform by sheer luck.

Conversation and applause punctuated the end of the
game.

Watching Neil leap over the net to claim his triumph, Bones consoled himself by thinking, I'd never have made it.

Neil was beaming as they walked off the courts. Yet, as if sensing Bones's disappointment, he said, "You kept me on my toes."

Gratefully, Bones returned his former opponent's smile. Tennis wasn't such a bad sport after all. Unlike baseball or basketball, you had to rely completely on your own skill to win, and now, even after he had lost the match, the memory of a net shot that he had reversed out of Neil's reach gave him satisfaction. That angle of reflection worked!

Instead of returning to Prue, Bones joined Hank.

As the seniors began their bout, Hank whispered, "You were in good form. You got three games off him. I don't think there's another guy in the intermediate division that would have come off as well against Neil."

Bones was comforted by Hank's words. He became aware of an element of success in his defeat.

The counselor continued: "Don't forget this is the first year you've taken tennis seriously. If you worked at it, you could beat Neil in a couple of years."

Bones leaned on his elbow and glanced sideways at Hank. "If I did nothing but play tennis all day, maybe," he replied.

Hank manipulated Bones's head toward the court. "Watch these guys. You might learn something."

"Did you teach them the angle of reflection, too?" Bones teased.

"Never mind," said Hank. "I noticed you used it, and you've learned enough now to be your own teacher."

When the tennis tournament was finished, the counselor sent Bones back to Prue, ordering him to stick with her.

Squid outdid himself at the next event, the track meet. He was so cocky while racing that he turned around every now and then to make donkey ears at his rivals.

Bones caught sight of Whitey as the campers headed for the girls' beach, the location of the cookout. "Wait up," he called.

"Hurry," Whitey ordered, "before they run out of hot dogs."

Pruneface sprinted down the track field after Bones. He wished he could lose her.

As they ran along the road past the Huber Building, Bones noted Updegraff's car parked in the woods. He wondered if the man was waiting for Chester. He must be, Bones concluded. Why else would he be here? But Chester was up ahead with Hank.

Dick had been correct in his description of the cookout. It *was* the best camp meal, and there was no cafeteria line, no limit to helpings of weiners, pickles, ice pops, soda, and marshmallows.

Even Pruneface was too busy stuffing herself to talk. Though a slender ballerina, she continued to gorge herself long after Bones had called a truce. She justified her fifteenth marshmallow by announcing, "I have a weak will."

Hank must be right. Your stomach does shrink, Bones thought, as he became aware of sharp pains in his abdomen.

He gave Whitey the high sign and walked toward him.

"Now's the time to escape, while they're all eating."

Whitey agreed, explaining that a songfest ended the cookout, and they would never be missed. Carefully, they edged toward the road, walking backwards until they reached the dirt trail. "Where do you want to go?" Whitey asked.

Bones wondered if Updegraff were still waiting for Chester. "My friend, the mackerel, was hanging around the Huber Building before. At least his car was there," Bones added. "Let's see what he's doing."

As they began to walk toward the drama cottage, Whitey said thoughtfully, "Funny he hangs around so much. He doesn't even have a kid in camp."

"Exactly," declared Bones. "That's what puzzles me. Let's kind of sneak up on him." He indicated a path in the woods.

"He's still there," Bones remarked, noticing that the black sports car was in its original parking space.

"I don't see anyone. Maybe he left his car with Chester for the day," Whitey speculated.

"He's probably in it, waiting."

"For Chester?"

"Who else?" Bones said impatiently. "I told you he's been meeting him on the sly."

"Meeting Chester at the Huber Building isn't meeting him on the sly. He probably just likes Chester."

"You are naïve," Bones announced with superiority. "No tycoon wastes this much time chatting with someone just because he likes him. I think he's using Chesty for some fishy purpose."

Whitey giggled. "You're obsessed with fish. Did your mother feed you striped bass instead of baby food?"

"Shush!" Bones warned, as the door of the Huber Building opened.

Updegraff and Chester walked down the steps and went to the car.

They watched the man hand the J.C. a large white laundry bag.

"Chester probably does his wash," Whitey murmured.

His arm hit a branch. The noise sounded like a firecracker in the stillness.

Bones pinched Whitey, then covered his friend's mouth before he could yell. "Quiet." Bones moved his lips without uttering a sound, while he watched the J.C. drag the laundry sack along the ground. It must be heavy, Bones realized, because Chesty was good at lifting weights.

Instead of going back into the building, Chester crawled underneath it and emerged empty-handed.

"You win." Whitey's mirth had disappeared. "Nobody puts dirty clothes under a house."

18. Updegraff's Hoard

The boys watched Updegraff manuever his car between the trees, crushing small bushes in his haste to reach the road. Chester brooded while the sports car zoomed away, leaving a trail of dust in its wake.

The J.C. moved slowly toward the dirt road. He stopped, sank his face into his hands, then lifted his head, heaved a long sigh, and continued in the direction of the cookout.

Silently the boys watched Chester's figure disappear.

Bones was the first to speak. "Whatever it is, Chester's not for it."

The laundry bag was waiting for them under the high side of the slope beneath the cottage.

"It might be dynamite," Whitey said in a tone that suggested caution.

"I know." Bones started to crawl under the building. It was a tight squeeze in spots.

Whitey did not follow him. "Let's get Hank."

Bones reached the bag and fingered it gingerly. It felt rigid under his touch, like a box. His palm curved around the side of the sack. He felt an uneven texture beneath the cloth that reminded him of coarse screening. Something had moved under his grasp!

Whitey had inched up to him. "What is it?"

"It's not dynamite," Bones announced with certainty. "It's something alive."

While the two boys stared, the bag seemed to be fluttering.

"It sure is lively!" Whitey exclaimed. "Maybe it's a wolf or a wildcat."

"I think there's a cage inside," Bones said. "But wild animals growl." He thought for a moment. "Let's poke it with a stick and see what kind of a noise comes out."

Each time they jabbed the bag it shook and emitted faint squeaks, but nothing howled.

Feeling braver, Bones bent down close to peer through the porous cloth. He heard a grating noise.

"Be careful," Whitey cautioned. "It might bite your head off."

"It sure looks like a cage." Bones pushed his face as close to the sack as he could without actually touching it. "Yep, it's a cage, and I think I see brown fur, too."

"Then it's not a skunk," declared Whitey. "And that's something to be grateful for."

"I don't think Updegraff meant us to be grateful for this present." Bones scratched his nose, then pulled his ear. "Do you suppose it could be a bear cub in hibernation?"

"Jerk! Bears hibernate in the winter!"

"Maybe this one is lazy," suggested Bones.

Whitey gave him an exasperated look.

"Well, we'll just have to open it up. If we don't go back soon, Pruneface will have the whole camp looking for us."

"I wish she would!" Whitey exclaimed. "I'd rather have my head chewed off with words than with teeth!"

Bones began to fiddle with the knot on top of the bag. Then he looked at Whitey. He saw fear mingled with fascination on his friend's face, a reflection of his own feelings.

"Don't you want to write your family a farewell note first?" Whitey asked.

Bones's curiosity overcame his fear of what the sack might hold. He would not be stopped. There was an animal in there all right, but it didn't sound like a man-eating lion, unless Updegraff had gagged it. This thought occurred to him just as the cord loosened.

In one daring movement, Bones pulled the bag apart. Without getting too close, he stared into it. His eyes bulged. Imprisoned in a wire mesh container, a mass of brown fur wiggled, and white teeth tried to gnaw their way to freedom.

"Rats!" he screamed. "Hundreds of them! Updegraff meant to turn them loose in the camp!" Suddenly Bones knew. "He's trying to ruin everything at Crescendo so he can buy the place cheap! The way he bought a hotel in Florida," he added, "when it was bankrupt!"

"How do you know all this?" Whitey appeared to doubt the explanation. Bones told him about his father's conversation with Updegraff the night of the play.

"But lots of people buy hotels when they're bankrupt," Whitey stated. "That doesn't prove anything here."

Bones bit his nails. "Let's get hold of Chester." He paused, then said, "No, wait. You stay here and mind the rats. I'll tackle Chester."

"What are you going to say to him?" Whitey asked.

"I'm gonna tell him we know what they're doing and—"

"But supposing they had no intention of letting the rats out at camp?"

"Then what are the rats doing here? Don't you see that if Updegraff didn't mean any harm, then the worst that can happen is that I'll sound like a nut. I'll make a fool of myself. But if my hunch is right, then we've got to stop them."

With a sigh of resignation, Whitey crouched down alongside of the rats. "I wish I had my transistor radio," he declared. "How long will this take?"

"Not long if I can locate Chester. Whatever happens," Bones warned, "wait for me."

"Don't forget about me," Whitey pleaded. "My neck is stiff from bending already."

"Move over." Bones pointed to where the incline below the building was steeper. "You don't have to get cosy with the rats."

19. Bones Points the Finger

Frowning, Chester stood apart from the group. He pounded a crumpled marshmallow box in his palm as if he were participating in the cleaning-up procedure. Oblivious to a nearby pair of campers who were swinging joined hands and blowing pink gum bubbles in rhythm, Chester rubbed his chin and stared at South Hill, a green slope in the distance.

Bones had arrived with a feeling of purpose, but when he saw the J.C., doubts replaced certainty. Maybe Whitey was right—maybe his imagination had allowed him to conjure up a story.

"Chester," he found himself saying.

The junior counselor turned around. He appeared startled, as if his thoughts had been miles away. His eyes focused on Bones, and he forced a smile. "It's you. Where's your date?"

Bones tried to put urgency into his voice. "I've got to speak to you alone."

Chester affected a puzzled look. Bones thought he detected the tenseness of distrust, but it was hard to tell. Chester was an actor. He felt uneasy waiting for the older boy to speak. Finally, in an attempt at nonchalance, the J.C. said, "No one is listening. You can speak here."

Bones shook his head. His thumb pointed toward the road. "Out there."

No one said anything as the boys walked away.

"Well?" Chester asked, upon reaching the main road.

Bones knew he had to assume the worst. There was no other way. "You and Updegraff have gone too far."

Chester stared at him, feigning perplexity, but this time the junior counselor's concern was apparent in the rigidity of his stance. His hands became fists, and the biceps of his upper arms bulged.

Chester's silence forced Bones into the aggressor's position. "I found the rats!"

"Rats?" The J.C.'s brow furrowed in an effort to sustain his innocent expression.

"And I saw you hide them under the Huber Building!"

A dumfounded look came over Chester. He started to run toward the drama cottage.

"Wait!" Bones called. "They're not there now!"

The J.C. stopped and wheeled around.

"I've hidden them," Bones lied.

Chester's fingers pinched Bones's shoulders. "Where are they?"

Bones decided to make the J.C. sweat. "I almost gave them to Uncle Willie," he said, "but I—"

"Where are they?" the counselor repeated, squeezing with more pressure.

"A friend of mine is guarding them. You'll never find them." Bones smirked, appreciating his own cleverness.

Chester appeared to believe him. His pretences vanished. "What are you going to do?" he cried.

Bones tried to speak with authority, to sound like his father. "It's not me that's going to do something. It's you."

"What do you expect me to do? Drown myself with the rats?"

Bones fingered his chin, unconsciously imitating his dad's gesture. "That's one way," he conceded. A trace of a smile accompanied his words.

The J.C. remained silent.

"You're in this up to your neck, aren't you?" Bones continued. He hazarded a guess. "You started the fire in the bus, and you fixed the boat so the rudder would come loose and there wouldn't be a paddle. What else did you do, paving the way for Updegraff to buy this place cheap?"

Chester was speechless. At last he said: "You're sharper than I thought. I'm responsible for all the things you mentioned, but," he added, "I haven't done anything else. *You'd* know it if I had."

"You didn't do a very good job with the fire," Bones couldn't help saying.

"Look," the J.C. replied, "Updegraff applied pressure. He guaranteed my future. He controls the most important repertory circuit in the country. He can virtually make or break a beginning actor, and so when he said I'd be a star in no time if I'd just—"

"Cooperate." Bones completed the sentence.

Chester heaved a sigh. "It was very tempting. Deep down I didn't expect his plan to work, but I thought if

I could go along with him for a while, that would satisfy him. A few practical jokes wouldn't wipe out Camp Crescendo, and in a sense I only cooperated halfheartedly. I could have poured gasoline on the bus."

"You could have used dynamite, too," Bones chided him.

"I wasn't out to kill anybody!" Chester defended himself.

"We might have drowned," Bones reminded him.

Chester's jaw fell. "I suppose I took a chance there, but," he reasoned, "you have to be a good swimmer to take out a boat, and the hull was fiberglass. It wouldn't have sunk."

"We might have tried to swim ashore."

"I didn't think of that," Chester admitted. "I just expected to stir up a scandal with a couple of kids missing for a few hours. You know," he gestured with his hands, "make things look like Crescendo didn't function properly."

"Does Updegraff always operate like this?"

"I wouldn't know." Chester's statement sounded honest. Bones did not press the subject.

"What difference does that make now?" There was a despairing note in Chester's voice. "By the time Updegraff decided to use rats, I had gone too far to back out."

Bones nodded gravely. "What are you going to do?"

"Leave. What else?" The J.C. threw up his hands.

"What will you say to Updegraff?"

"I don't plan to see Updegraff," Chester announced with finality. The J.C. sighed and continued, "In a way, I'm glad you stopped me, but I wish *you* hadn't been the one to catch me."

"You mean because of Carolyn."

Chester nodded. "If I could just have run away—"

"But, you wouldn't," Bones interrupted. He tried to argue some sense into the older boy. "Look, you can still run away if you want to or you can—"

"Confess like a man, and then leave." Chester's voice cracked as he spoke, betraying the emotional upheaval he was going through. "I feel like a fool." He hid his face in the bend of his arm.

It was easier to face an arrogant Chesty than a contrite one. "Look," said Bones, "they say Uncle Willie is a saint. Tell him the truth, and see what he suggests."

"I couldn't." The J.C. moaned.

"He'll keep your secret. That much I know."

Bones had spoken with certainty, and Chester looked partially convinced.

"Why did this have to happen? I was just beginning to enjoy myself here. Beginning to feel as if I was accomplishing something," the junior counselor said ruefully.

A while back Bones would have been glad to see Chester in a mess like this. Now it troubled him. Chester had a tough shell, but he was responding to the atmosphere at Crescendo. He was beginning to find pleasure in his job, and slowly the boys in the cabin had come to respect, yes, even like their J.C.

Silently, Bones and Chester, each involved in his own thoughts, started back toward the campfire in search of Uncle Willie. Bones supported Chesty with an encouraging smile.

When they arrived, the party was ending. Girls were heading for the cabins to change for the swimming meet, and the boys were being hustled toward the buses.

Hank spotted Bones and motioned to him.

"I'll come back with Chesty," Bones called.

The director stood talking with Paul, the head swimming instructor, and one of the girl counselors. Bones stopped, folded his arms, and waited for the J.C. to move forward alone.

Chester gave Bones a pleading look. Sweat glistened on his forehead, and his hands trembled. "It's like walking up to the electric chair," he said—but he went.

Bones watched Uncle Willie and Chester walk toward main camp. They'll probably go to the director's office, he surmised, following them at a distance.

Bones was correct. He watched the two enter the building where Uncle Willie's office was located. When the door shut, he sat down in the wooded area nearby. He rested against a pine tree and remembered Whitey. Poor guy. He was probably talking to those rats by now, but Bones had to wait. He had to be with Chester when he disposed of the rats.

Little by little, doubt trickled through Bones. I should have gone with him, he told himself. Yet he knew his presence would have made Chester's position more awkward. It would have been as though he were monitoring the junior counselor's confession. His uneasiness increased. What was to stop Chester from making up a story? Supposing he told the director I brought in the rats!

20. Chester Takes the Lead

Bones brushed aside his suspicions of Chester. He would soon know what was taking place in the director's office.

Leaning against the tree trunk with his head tilted back, Bones's eyes traveled upward to the top branches of the pine forest. The pine needles intermeshed as in etchings, screening the blue sky and the scattered clouds, and reminding him of a stage set. It was a moment of tranquility, one of the rare times that Bones had been left alone at camp with nothing to do but think.

When he had first arrived at Crescendo, he had marveled at the change that camp made in Whitey's personality. At home, Whitey, a nonathletic, quiet boy, took a back seat; here, as first flutist in the camp orchestra, he came alive. Quite the opposite seemed to be taking place within Chester; he had come to camp prepared to fight the world, and now he was losing his belligerence. There was something about the camp setting that was different from the school scene. Maybe, Bones thought, this was because you didn't have to be an athlete, a comedian, or a showoff to gain status at Crescendo. He couldn't imagine any of his friends trying out for a Shakespearean play at school, and yet he had enjoyed being Bottom—in spite of the costume. At camp, no matter what your interest was, it was respected as long as you worked at it. At home, if you tried too hard, you were considered a grind.

Bones realized that Chester had appeared to straighten out after his success as the Champion. The kids had appreciated his talent and voiced their admiration, much to the J.C.'s surprise. Suddenly, Chester wasn't fighting anyone. Everyone was on his side.

Bones had a hunch he had acted properly, and Chester would come through in the end. Now he understood that Uncle Willie's speech on the first night of camp was not just propaganda. Living at Crescendo could make you a better person, but it took a summer here to become aware of this.

Bones heard the door open. He became alert.

Chester emerged alone.

Bones stood waiting for the J.C. to meet him in the protection of the woods. When Chester confronted him, all his doubts vanished. The older boy looked limp; his cheeks were yellow instead of tan. His eyes had an odd expression, too. He seemed dazed, yet not completely beaten.

"What took you so long?"

Chesty's mouth widened into a puzzled half-smile. "You

were right. Uncle Willie is a saint." He paused for a moment, shook his head in wonder, and added, "Or else he's a lunatic."

"What happened?"

Chester replied simply, "He heard my story, and he asked me to stay."

Bones glowed inwardly. His intuition had not deceived him. "I'm not surprised," he stated at last. "What did he say?"

"His words are glued to my brain," said Chester. "He told me that 'although promoting the arts is important at Crescendo, it is secondary to character building.' He said, 'The greater the error, the more difficult the confession.' He told me that I was courageous to come to him and that he wanted to confirm my faith in him by letting me clear up the matter myself."

Chester's eyes met Bones's. "He put the fate of the camp in my hands!"

Bones caught his breath and meditated a moment. Then he spoke with conviction. "When a guy like that has confidence in you, you do the right thing."

"Exactly." Chester's eyes were shining. "I'm not used to that kind of generosity. It makes me feel worse than if he'd kicked me out. And it makes me want to do some good around here."

There was a new warmth in Chester's voice. Uncle Willie had been smart, Bones mused. By placing the responsibility in Chesty's lap, he had given the J.C. a chance to prove that his confession had meaning.

Suddenly Bones remembered Whitey. "What happens to the rats?"

Chester snickered. "I'll have to face Hubert after all. He'll have to cart away his little friends. Where are they, anyway?" he asked curiously.

Bones chuckled, then caught Chester's eye, and replied, "Under the Huber Building."

Stunned, Chester cried, "You didn't hide them?"

"Nope."

"You mean I could have got rid of them without a confession!"

Bones could not refrain from giggling while he jabbed the J.C.'s shoulder in a gesture of friendship. "Aren't you glad you confessed?"

"You little stinker!" the boy declared, but he didn't look angry. "You're gonna be just like Uncle Willie when you grow up!"

Bones started to run. "We'd better rescue Whitey. He's probably fallen asleep with the rats! Good thing we're not in the swimming meet," he added.

The next morning Chester went with Bones when he asked for permission to miss his swim period. Bones explained that the J.C. needed help at the Huber Building. And in a way this was true, for Chester was expecting Mr. Updegraff between eleven-thirty and noon, a time when no drama classes were scheduled. He hustled Bones inside the cottage, cautioning him to remain hidden, while he sat on the steps outside waiting for the black sports car.

The screeching of brakes and the sound of a door slamming informed Bones of the man's arrival. Bones slid along the wall toward the window and peeked outside. The two were talking, their backs to him. Bones remained rigid. His heart thumped so loudly that he was afraid Hubert Updegraff would detect him. Wide-eyed, he watched Chester hand the rats to Updegraff. He couldn't see the man's face, but there were no sounds of protest.

Hubert Updegraff hauled the laundry sack along the

ground, then lifted it and shoved it onto the red leather seat in the rear of his sports car.

A mighty elegant conveyance for rats, Bones thought. He noticed that this time the man did not dally to chat with his former protégé, but raced his motor impatiently and sped away without so much as a good-by glance.

Bones raised the window and climbed out, landing with a thud. "What did you say to him?" he asked.

"I told him the villain in his drama quit after having been found out." Chester laughed. "I didn't tell him it was a camper who stopped me, but I told him we were lucky to get off so easily."

"You were."

"Yeah," Chester continued "He agreed. He has a reputation to safeguard, too." The J.C. stuck his hands in his pockets and raised his shoulders. "He couldn't understand Uncle Willie letting me off the hook. I think he's convinced I'm making up the whole thing." Chester looked down. Shaking his head, he said, "But he didn't press me."

"He could see that your mind was made up."

"And it is," Chesty remarked with determination. "I'm starting college in the fall, and I'll go with a clean slate." He was silent a minute and then said, "I might try out for summer stock next year, but if I do, I'll steer clear of the Updegraff circuit."

"You're a good actor on your own. You don't need any help from him," Bones said with honesty.

Chester winked at Bones. "Thanks," he said, "but it's not as easy as you think."

21. No Sweet Substitutes

Uncle Willie's decision brought about a pact between Bones and Whitey. Because the director meant to give Chester a second chance, the boys felt bound to carry out his wishes. They must not, even by suggestion, cause anyone else to learn the nature of Chester's tie with Updegraff. Bones informed the J.C. of their plan, adding that even Carolyn would never know unless he chose to tell her himself.

As the days passed, the combined effect of Chester's parting from Updegraff and Uncle Willie's kindness changed the J.C.'s relationship with his cabin mates. His goading, which had become less frequent, stopped altogether. Following Hank's example, Chester put himself out to give the boys a good time and to draw Neil into comradeship with the group. In the early evenings, he took the boys fishing. In the period before taps, he read them tales by Poe and stories about Sherlock Holmes. He made them shiver in suspense and huddle beneath the sheets while he dramatized each awe-inspiring climax, and they loved it.

During that last wonderful week at Crescendo, Bones realized the fun of camp could never be understood by leafing through a catalogue. Nor could it be explained to his father in words. It was the seemingly unimportant things—Hank's interest in his diet, Chesty's bedtime readings, trying to win games from Neil in informal tennis matches, and just being with the other fellows—that gave most to the summer. Uncle Willie had spoken the truth when he said progress in the arts was only a small part of camp life.

On the last day, the boys packed silently. Even Squid looked somber. He put a lanky arm across Bones's shoulder and said wistfully, "I wish I could take you home with me."

"We'll get together in the winter," Bones replied. "We'll have a reunion. You bring the syrup."

Leafy taped the lids of his lotions, looking morose and downhearted. He came from Boston and lived the farthest away.

Whitey put a hand on Treehurst's shoulder. "You can spend the weekend with me."

"And Neil can stay with me," Bones said, "if he can stand living with Midge."

The boys laughed.

Hank stuck his fingers underneath the waistband of Bones's shorts. "You plan to gain it all back tonight at the banquet?" he joshed.

"How can I?" Bones retorted. "You murdered my appetite!"

"Guess your mother's cooking will restore it," Hank said knowingly.

"Not if my father can help it!" Bones exclaimed. "Once he offered me a dollar for every pound I lost!"

Dick whistled. "You'd better gorge tonight, so you can go home and get rich!"

"It's people like your father who make the Wirtz Syrup Company lose money," Squid commented.

Hank walked between the bunk beds, rotating his shoulders in a hustling motion. "C'mon fellas, let's clean up," he urged.

Flip and Tony began to tear pictures of sport heroes from the walls.

Squid placed himself in front of the calendar girl above his bed, yelling, "She's coming home with me!"

The boys looked at each other in mock wonder, then they tapped their heads.

"He's sick," Tony stated.

They moved on, stripping the walls of pennants and pictures.

Chesty squatted on a trunk and eyed the thumbtacks that had been tossed into a cracked plastic glass in the center of the floor. "There was a time when I would have been afraid to sit down with all this ammunition floating around," he jested.

Momentarily, a devilish gleam sparkled in Squid's eyes. Then he shrugged his bony shoulders. "It's no fun teasing you any more. You don't get mad."

Simultaneously, Hank and Bones glanced at Chester to observe his reaction to Squid's remark. The J.C. rewarded them with a smug smile and a wink.

Without being told, the boys made themselves neat for

the last camp dinner—the farewell banquet. Their shiny
faces beamed in anticipation of the evening's festivities,
and, temporarily, the sorrow that came with the knowl-
edge that they would soon part was forgotten.

"Ah's" of admiration accompanied the arrival of the
campers on the scene of the feast. Pungent-smelling pine
boughs hung from the rafters of the recreation hall.
Cloth-covered tables, arranged in a long crescendo sign,
stretched across the room. At the point of the crescendo,
which separated the boy and girl campers, Uncle Willie
stood and greeted them, obviously pleased by the excited
faces.

The tables were lined up according to cabin number.
The boys in Cabin Eight found their table quickly. Their
individual seats were determined by a descriptive ditty
lying on top of a maple sugar crescendo sign.

In search of his seat, Bones chuckled. He went from
place to place, reading:

> *He won the race like cracking eggs,*
> *Our boy, this laughing face on legs.*

> *At seven A.M. with his brazen blare*
> *He spoils our dreams, but what does he care?*

> *Though he didn't make concert master,*
> *This tinkerer can cause disaster.*

> *In his own quiet way, he is astute,*
> *This tow-haired fellow who plays first flute.*

> *He better stick to being "jivey,"*
> *Instead of painting poison ivy.*

Can't see his whizzing aces.
This guy is going places.

Finally he reached his own and read:

He came to this camp with flesh to spare.
Now his mother will faint 'cause he's Bone *bare!*

Following the example of the others, Bones waited for
Uncle Willie to say grace before sitting down. A hush
settled over the room, and the campers looked at the director, anxious for him to begin.

The hall was silent even after Uncle Willie's words.
With reverence the youngsters watched platters of fried
chicken and corn-on-the-cob being carried into the room.
Memories of chipped beef, creamed hash, and rubbery
eggs faded, replaced by the abundance of the last camp
dinner.

It was the dessert, however, that crowned the feast.
Murmurs of delight ushered in the baked Alaskas, their
white puffs of meringue toasted golden brown. Tenderly,
Hank touched the peaked crust with his knife. Then he
eyed Bones.

He's not going to give me any, Bones thought, watching
Hank slice a generous portion.

Grinning, the counselor said, "The Spartan over there
gets the first piece." He handed the plate to Bones.

Bones's mouth watered as he stared down at the melting
stripes of chocolate and vanilla ice cream beneath the
brown-tinged white topping.

When all the boys had been served, Hank glanced at
Bones once more and remarked, "Oh, wait a minute. I
forgot—"

Bones held on to his plate with both hands, but the

counselor did not reach for it. Instead, Hank excused himself from the table.

It was customary to eat dessert as a group. The boys waited impatiently for their leader to return. All eyes were fastened to their plates. All spoons were clutched, ready to attack.

"For you," Hank announced, setting a can of Wirtz Syrup in front of Bones.

"Ha, ha!" Bones chuckled victoriously, while he dripped the syrup over his ice cream until the entire top was covered with chocolate lava. "Vesuvius has just erupted!" he declared with delight. To appear less of a pig, he passed the can to Whitey and said, "You kids can have the rest."

When the plates had been scraped and the boys were leaning back, Uncle Willie rose. "Time for the awards."

In general, the campers knew what plaques they would receive. Now they continued to relax, munching or sucking chunks of maple candy, while the director called out the activities and the counselors presented the medals.

Bones clapped when Neil accepted his tennis award. Squid earned one for track. Whitey and others, who had first chairs in band or orchestra, won awards for merit in music. Bones expected no tangible prize himself. He would be wearing his achievement home in the form of missing inches. He pushed away the remainder of his maple sugar crescendo. No point in gaining all his loss or losing all his gains in one meal.

"The fishing award," announced Uncle Willie.

Much to Cabin Eight's surprise, Chester stood up to make the presentation. The J.C. wasn't a waterfront counselor. The boys cocked their heads curiously.

The junior counselor beamed and said, "Goes to—" he paused for effect, rolled his eyes until they rested on

Bones, and exclaimed, "—to Boniface Cluett, for catching a sixteen-inch pike!"

Bones turned purple. Before him lay the trophy, a small fish hooked to a brass crescendo sign that was mounted on a mahogany board. Chester was giving him an award for the fish he had slipped into the J.C.'s bed. Bones looked at Whitey, who was facing the ceiling and gnawing his knuckles. Then he scanned the room. The whole camp was waiting for him to shake hands with the J.C., thereby accepting his honor.

Bones stood leaning against the table for support. Chester's act had obviously been an offering of friendship, and he wanted the J.C. to know he appreciated it. The problem was that Bones had not caught the pike. How could he tell him this? he wondered.

"Didn't know Rainbow Lake had anything but sunfish," Uncle Willie stated, while Bones groped for words.

Bones gripped a fork between his fingers and addressed Chester. "I presented you with the pike, but I didn't have the honor of catching it," he said somberly. "It was Whitey's bite!"

Chester's jaw dropped. He stared blankly at Hank. "I never thought of that."

The senior counselor looked at Bones, then leaned back in his chair and roared until the tears rolled down his cheeks.

Now Bones knew that they had been buddies in this gag.

When Hank's laughter had subsided, Uncle Willie declared, "Such honesty deserves another award, but since we don't have one, all I can say is that your words were spoken in the true Crescendo tradition."

Bones walked away from the banquet meditatively. He was certain that Hank Fulweiler had instructed the J.C.

to ignore the fish incident. Actually, the senior counselor, with his sense of fair play, had paved the way for Chesty's break with Updegraff, for if their J.C. had really been determined to turn the rats loose in the camp, two little squirts couldn't have stopped him!

He caught up with Chesty. "Thanks for being such a good sport about the fish!"

"The least I could do after what you've done for me."

"It wasn't me," Bones protested modestly. "It was Uncle Willie with his second chance—and Hank, too, in a way."

"They helped," Chester conceded. "All the people you live with, at least the ones who are interested in you, affect the way you behave," he explained. "But, skinny Bones, I'm most grateful to you." His hand squeezed Bones's shoulder. It was a brotherly touch—what Hank might have done, and Bones sensed the J.C.'s good will.

"Don't you see?" Chester persisted. "All you had to do was take the rats to Uncle Willie and I was a goner!"

"I never really considered doing that," Bones admitted.

"No, you offered me a chance to square myself instead. And because you didn't squeal, because you came to me, I *knew* I had to face the judge."

Bones's chest expanded. Chester's gratitude hit deeper than a barrage of medals. Now more than ever he was pleased that he had curbed his tongue and kept Chesty's secret. His summer at camp had not turned him into a musician, but he had discovered something he would never forget. By watching Uncle Willie in action, Bones had learned that a risk involving human worth repays the gambler!

His eyes met the older boy's. "I'm glad everything worked out."

"It must have," Chester agreed with pride, "because

Uncle Willie has asked me to come back to Crescendo next year!"

"That's great!" exclaimed Bones. An impish giggle slipped out as he added, "If you don't ever make me wear bloomers again!"

"We'll wrap you up in the future," the J.C. promised. "There's always *St. George and the Dragon.* How would you like to be covered with scales?"

Bones sighed comfortably and blinked up at the star-studded sky. Next summer seemed as far away as the Little Dipper.

"Funny, Chesty," he said as they walked toward the bus, "I never thought I'd like you."

Caryl, Jean   jW
  Bones and the smiling
                    mackerel.

Redwood Library and Athenaeum

NEWPORT, R. I.

Selections from the Rules

New fiction is issued for 7 days, new non-fiction for 14 days, and other books for 28 days with the privilege of renewal.

Books overdue are subject to a fine of 2 cents a day.

All injuries to books and all losses shall be made good to the satisfaction of the Librarian.

5 volumes may be taken at a time and only 5 on 1 share or subscription.

LIBRARY BUREAU CAT. NO. 1166.3